The Seven

Fred Ellis Brock

Pub Date: June 2020

ISBN: 978-1-948018-77-7 Trade Paperback
212 pages, 5.5 x 8.5, $15.95

CATEGORIES:
FIC031000 Thrillers
FIC024000 Supernatural
FIC028000 Science Fiction
FIC028010 Science Fiction/Action & Adventure

DISTRIBUTED BY:
INGRAM, FOLLETT, COUTTS, MBS, YBP,
COMPLETE BOOK, BERTRAMS, GARDNERS
Or wholesale@wyattmackenzie.com

Wyatt-MacKenzie Publishing
DEADWOOD, OREGON

PUBLISHER CONTACT:
Nancy Cleary
nancy@wyattmackenzie.com

AGENT CONTACT:
Deborah Hofmann, David Black Literary Agency
DHofmann@dblackagency.com

AUTHOR CONTACT:
Fred Brock
feb2@mac.com

THE SEVEN

THE SEVEN

THE FIRST BOOK IN THE SEVEN TRILOGY

FRED ELLIS BROCK

The Seven

Fred Ellis Brock

The First Novel in THE SEVEN Trilogy

ISBN: 978-1-948018-77-7 Trade Paperback
LCCN: *to come*

The characters and events in this book are fictitious. Any similarity to real persons, living or dead, is coincidental and not intended by the author.

Wyatt-MacKenzie Publishing, Inc., Deadwood, OR
www.wyattmackenzie.com

PROLOGUE

Washington County, Indiana: New Year's Day, 1952

Fran Jamison awoke and sat up on the edge of the bed, pulling the covers around her shoulders for a few extra seconds of warmth. The sun was just coming up, and she was anxious to get started on New Year's Day dinner. Joe, her husband, grunted and rolled over as she stood and began to dress in the cold, semi-dark room. Pulling the curtain aside from the east-facing window nearest the bed, she could see that a fresh layer of snow had fallen during the night, giving the flat land around the farmhouse a cold sparkling beauty in the slanting sunlight. She opened the bedroom door and quietly walked down the upstairs hall, toward the bathroom and past a room shared by her twin daughters and another room that was her son's. The door to the boy's room was partly open; she glanced at Joey's form under several quilts and paused to listen to his gentle snoring.

A few minutes later Fran was downstairs in the kitchen, making a batch of biscuits for breakfast. In the refrigerator was a turkey, ready to go into the oven when the biscuits were done. The radio was on and the Salem station was playing a Hank Williams song she hadn't heard before.

Fran was at the sink filling the percolator with water when the morning brightness dimmed as if a cloud had passed in front of the sun. Suddenly, she felt queasy. The sounds of the radio and the running water seemed low and distant, as though she had cotton in her ears. But in less than a minute the sunlight and sounds returned to normal. She sat the coffee pot in the bottom of the sink and slumped into a kitchen chair, a wave of weakness passing over her.

A few seconds later, terrible feelings of foreboding and dread welled up, unexplained, from Fran's stomach. Her hands shook, and perspiration streamed down her face.

She jumped up, dashed from the kitchen and up the stairs, taking them two at a time. When she reached the upstairs hallway, she saw the door to Joey's room was shut. The bathroom door was standing open, just as she had left it earlier. She opened Joey's door, saw his empty bed and began to scream.

"What the hell? Frannie?" Joe mumbled as he lurched from his bed. He was unable to find his robe and, clad in his undershorts, rushed into the hall. Fran's screams had also awakened the twins, who ran, panicked, into the hall, four identical green eyes wide with fright.

Joe grabbed Fran by the arms and began to shake her. "What is it?" he shouted. "What's the matter?"

Fran's screams dropped down into choking sobs. "Joey's gone!" she gasped. "Something's happened to Joey!"

Joe turned and burst into Joey's room, flicking on the overhead light. Joey's jeans and red flannel shirt were hanging on a chair beside his empty bed. His shoes were under the chair. Joe walked over to the window. It was locked from the inside. Through the partially frosted pane, he could see a field of undisturbed snow below. As if suddenly deaf, Fritz, the family's German shepherd, was sleeping soundly on a rug at the foot of Joey's bed.

For the next half hour the four frantically searched everywhere in the house for Joey. Joe even went up into the attic and down into the basement; finally, he went outside. He found nothing but a blanket of untouched snow. No footprints except his own. No tracks of any kind. There was nothing in the barn except the family Ford, some hay, and two milk cows.

Joe called the Sheriff's office in Salem. The Sheriff, suspicious of Joe's account of the boy's disappearance, questioned the parents for more than an hour while deputies searched and house and barn. Later in the day, the Sheriff spoke to witnesses who had seen Joey and his mother at the IGA grocery in Salem the afternoon before he was missing. They appeared perfectly normal. The Sheriff, who had known the Jamison family for years, quickly dismissed any suspicions he had about Joe and Fran.

For the next two weeks police and volunteers combed the countryside for miles around the Jamison farmhouse, checking every barn, outbuilding, wooded area, and ravine. Icy ponds were dragged. Scores of people questioned. Eleven-year-old Joey Jamison had simply vanished.

On the second Sunday of the month, a prayer service for the missing boy was held at the Salem Methodist Church. Many years later both his parents went to their graves never knowing what happened to their son.

*

The White House, Washington: Friday, December 19, 1980

Jimmy Carter, alone in the Oval Office, sat in a dusty-rose, wing-backed chair in front of a gently burning fire. A maroon file folder lay in his lap. He could barely hear the muffled sound of sleet pelting the thick, bulletproof windows that looked onto the South Lawn. He had just finished eating lunch at his desk and within the hour was scheduled to hold a third and final two-hour meeting with President-elect Ronald Reagan. Carter dreaded the meeting. He and Reagan didn't like each other and were barely able to conceal it. Carter was annoyed at Reagan's inability to grasp the simplest ideas the departing president had tried to discuss. *He has the attention span of a gnat.* Carter was annoyed with himself that he couldn't clear his mind of the meeting and concentrate on something else. *Well, at least it'll be over in two hours. Then they can swear him in next month and he can worry about the hostages. If he can concentrate long enough to worry.*

Carter stared at the fireplace and let his mind drift. He remembered his amused surprise when he moved into the

White House four years ago and discovered that the heating and cooling systems were so sophisticated that the fireplace in the Oval Office didn't draw naturally like a normal fireplace—the smoke had to be pumped out by hidden exhaust fans. If they weren't turned on before a fire was started, smoke would fill the room.

A log popped, causing Carter to start and knock the folder from his lap onto the blue-carpeted floor. He leaned over and picked it up. Only the title page, the first of eleven pages, had partially slipped from the file. He studied the title: "A Summary of Three Reports on the Pine Bush Phenomenon." "EYES ONLY – THE PRESIDENT, COPY 1 (ONE) OF 1 (ONE)," was stamped above the title and on each of the single-spaced, hand-typed and numbered pages. Each page, as well as the front of the folder, carried the imprint of the National Security Agency.

Carter reread the file's contents for the third time that day. It only raised his irritation level. He knew the pages were filled with lies. And he knew there was nothing he could do about it. What he didn't know was why. Why, whenever he asked for a summary or a report dealing with this subject, was he given lies? Prompt. Well-prepared. Documented. But lies. Presented to him in such a way that they couldn't be disputed or challenged. Not without him looking like a kook.

Carter knew he should discuss the file with Reagan. He stared at it in his right hand. Then he stood, opened the fireplace screen and threw the folder and its pages onto the burning logs. *He'll find out soon enough. If he can stay awake that long. Or maybe he'll never figure it out. Or maybe it doesn't matter. Maybe there's nothing that can be done anyway.* He watched the pages and the file folder burn to ash. Then he walked over to his desk and signed a logbook, carefully adding the date and time. His signature certified that he had personally destroyed the file.

A quiet knock on the curved door leading to his secretary's office told him that Reagan's motorcade was pulling into the north portico of the White House.

*

Ulster County, New York: The Present

The log cabin was nestled deep in the woods in the center of a two-hundred-acre tract of land in Ulster County, about fifteen miles north of the little town of Pine Bush in neighboring Orange County. The cabin wasn't visible from the macadam road that ran along the west side of the property. If a curious stranger were to drive down the rutted, unpaved gravel road leading to the cabin, he or she would be greeted by a friendly, white-haired man chopping wood in a small clearing to the front of the log structure. The old man would chat for a bit about how he and his wife—she would be off buying groceries—liked the solitude there after a career spent eighty-five miles south in New York City, where he had worked as a stockbroker for a major Wall Street firm. If necessary, he could easily slip into a conversation about the latest market trends or promising stocks.

When the stranger drove back to the paved road, he or she wouldn't notice, as hadn't been noticed during the drive in, that every move was being tracked by hidden cameras and sophisticated electronic sensors buried in the ground and carefully camouflaged in trees and on fence posts. The cabin, the woodcutter, the logs, even the smoke curling from the stone chimney, were all part of an elaborate set, more sophisticated than anything ever devised by Disneyland or Hollywood. It was there to conceal what lay underground. The cabin hid an elevator that descended to the entrance of a gigantic subterranean bunker with living quarters for twenty people. Branching off the bunker were connecting chambers crammed with electronic equipment, including two advanced Chinese Sunway supercomputers.

Retired Colonel Richard West leaned heavily on his cane as he eased into an overstuffed chair in his office beneath the cabin. He knew he was dying and was glad to be back in the cool semi-darkness of this familiar room after a trip to Langley that had left him drained.

We don't really know any more now than we did when Truman started this whole business. We've made a lot of guesses, and that's all. This may lead to nothing. Or create more mystery. Goddamn! I want to understand what the hell is going on more than I've ever wanted anything. If we don't—or can't—understand, what's the point of the deceptions, the ruined lives, the deaths?

But Richard West knew one thing for certain even as more questions formed in his mind: Absolute secrecy had to be maintained.

CHAPTER 1

Bill Sanders was running hard down a crowded airport concourse, trying to reach Jane and stop her before she got on the plane. Suddenly he was running in slow motion and people were blocking his path with suitcases and baby carriages. An old man in a wheelchair plowed into Bill, deliberately knocking him down. Seeing his victim on the floor, the old man's mouth of crooked yellow teeth grimaced in an exaggerated glow of sinister self-satisfaction, a look captured more brightly under high-wattage fluorescent lights.

The end of the concourse, where Jane was in a crowd of people boarding an Air France flight for New York, receded into the distance. Now Bill could see the crowd through the wrong end of a telescope. Then he was screaming at an airline official who seemed unable to hear him. LISTEN TO ME, GODDAMMIT! THERE'S A BOMB ON THAT AIRPLANE! A BOMB! The word echoed down a sterile steel corridor. Then Bill heard the hissing of a closing pneumatic door. The official looked at him and smiled. "I'm sorry sir, but that flight is already on the runway and ready to take off. It cannot be stopped at this time. It cannot be stopped at this time. It cannot be stopped. It cannot ...."

Bill jerked awake in a cold sweat. His heart pounded as the recurring dream remained sharp in his mind. Car lights outside a window momentarily confused him until he remembered that he was in a motel room along Interstate 70, a few miles east of Columbus, Ohio. He turned on the bedside light and looked at his watch. Five-thirty. The dream's images began to break apart and fade, replaced by thoughts of Paul and his plea for help that had drawn Bill west.

He lay back and replayed the previous day in his mind. The New York taxi driver who talked nonstop about how much he missed his family in Ghana as he drove Bill to the Port Authority bus terminal. The surly bus driver who gave him a lecture when he asked to be let off between regular stops in Montclair, New Jersey. Each step of the four-block walk to the Hertz office was almost pleasant by comparison, even with the drag of his duffel bag as it pulled downward on his right shoulder, along with the weight of a backpack stuffed with several books and a laptop computer. He had started renting cars in New Jersey so that he could avoid driving in the maddeningly heavy New York City traffic. The rentals were also cheaper than in Manhattan, which he had discovered last year during a brief affair with a high school teacher who lived in Montclair. Remembering her brought a stab of pain, and shame. He hadn't been ready for a relationship and handled it badly.

He was in the car and on the road by nine, heading south on the Garden State Parkway, west on Interstate 78 to Allentown, Pennsylvania, down the Northeast extension of the Pennsylvania Turnpike to Valley Forge, and then west on the turnpike. The Saturday traffic was light; he skirted Pittsburgh, had a late fast-food lunch at a turnpike rest stop and rolled into Ohio. The land flattened into fields of dark, rich soil that were being plowed for spring planting.

Bill always felt lighter as he drove west, away from the congestion and hustle of the East Coast. As usual when he traveled, he fantasized about what it would be like to live wherever he was. This time, he thought of moving back to the Midwest. Maybe back to Jefferson.

The emotion of the airport dream that haunted Bill several times a month faded. Over the past two years he often thought of seeing a psychiatrist, but rejected the idea as an invasion of his privacy. He simply didn't want to talk about his reaction to Jane's death with anyone. Not yet. Maybe never.

His mind drifted back to Wednesday and lunch with Nancy Luke, his agent. He had returned to New York the previous Sunday from a month-long trip to rural areas of Vietnam and Cambodia where he was researching a travel piece that would be a central chapter in an anthology a friend was editing. The Asia trip had been a good excuse to get out of New York for a while. The call from Paul came Tuesday night; Bill mentioned it briefly when Nancy called him Wednesday morning to confirm their lunch.

Her first question, after they were seated and ordered drinks, was, "Jefferson, Indiana? Where's that?"

Bill remembered mentally grimacing. Nancy was an Upper East Side New Yorker whose sense of United States geography from west of the Hudson River to California was more than a little vague. She had been Bill's literary agent for ten years and was one of the four or five best in New York. Their author-agent relationship was based on a bedrock of success and money. Nancy wrangled Bill the best advances and book contracts she could from publishers and got fifteen percent off the top. But in the beginning, when Bill had quit his reporting job to write books and was having little success and making no money, she stuck with him and believed in him. Although she did so out of pure self-interest, he would never forget it. They both recognized they were not close friends, that their relationship was essentially professional. They seldom discussed anything personal. She was too guarded and self-protective—detached, some called her—and Bill had never had any reason to want to break through her defenses. The central axes of their lives could never cross: she grew up in New York, Martha's Vineyard, and Europe, the only child of a man who had made twenty million dollars by the time he was thirty, and was married to a senior partner in one of the top-earning law firms in New York; Bill grew up dirt poor, one of two sons of a hard-scrabble Midwestern farmer and his wife, and had feelings of insecurity about the money he had made, as if it weren't real or might evaporate at any moment, leaving only a faint green memory. He suffered through interviews and books parties that Nancy and his publisher arranged for him. As he mingled, he was often aware that he was almost certainly the only person in the room who had ever lived in a trailer or whose family had had a car repossessed. As he held a pen to autograph books, he often wondered if his were the only set of knuckles that had been skinned getting a balky tractor started. Had any of the guests ever worried that a crop-damaging spring hailstorm might drive their father to the county welfare office? His motivations to succeed were clear; Nancy's were subtler, rooted in a sense of family standards and responsibilities.

"It's the town nearest …."

Gerald, the white-jacketed waiter who usually served them, interrupted to bring oversized Bloody Marys that had seemed perfect for a warm April afternoon. But the drinks looked a bit comical with their too-tall, leafy shafts of celery. The restaurant, Dave's, was a little more pretentious than the food was good, but Bill and Nancy met there for more or less regular monthly lunches because it was midway between her office near Rockefeller Center and his apartment on East Seventy-Second Street. Nancy liked Dave's because it wasn't a regular hangout for authors and agents, many eavesdropping for gossip and information. Nancy said some agents paid waiters in those haunts to keep their eyes and ears open.

"… to where I grew up in Southern Indiana, on the Ohio River. I've told you before. It's where I had my first newspaper job at The Jefferson Courier. You don't remember because it's not between the Hudson and East rivers."

Nancy wrinkled her nose and made a funny face as she reached for a saltshaker. Her geographic shortcomings were a running joke between them, as was his struggle to deal with Google Maps, GPS devices, and technology in general. His work had forced him to master a computer, but that was about it. He was wary of electronic devices that had to be upgraded every six months. His friends sometimes teased him for being a Luddite because he still carried a flip phone. But as a veteran reporter, he knew enough about the dark side of technology to be leery of most current electronic devices that could track an owner's every move. The Internet was a great tool for gathering information and data, but it worked both ways. Plus, he simply liked words on paper: books, notes, maps.

"And you're going there to help a childhood friend you haven't seen in years? You don't know what his problem is, and you don't know how long you'll be gone? When are you're leaving?"

The waiter returned for their orders. Both had Cobb salad, the Wednesday special. As the waiter took their menus, Bill's thoughts drifted back to a fishing and camping trip he and Paul had taken when they were juniors at Jefferson High School. They hadn't caught any fish and lived for three days on baloney and crackers.

"Saturday morning. I'm going to rent a car in New Jersey and drive out."

"What's the man's name again?"

"Paul. Paul Watson. He's a high school guidance counselor. In Jefferson."

"And you haven't seen him since you were in high school? Or was it college?"

"College, almost. Actually, we did meet a couple of times after college. And at the funerals of my mom and dad. And he and his wife, Sharon, once visited me here. We've stayed in touch. We talk on the phone three or four times a year. He and Sharon were coming to Jane's funeral but couldn't because Paul's father got really sick. His mother had died a year earlier."

"Is he in some kind of trouble? Why would he ask you for help after all these years?"

"I'm not sure. He was in a panic when he called and said there was no one else who could help him. He would only tell me it was urgent and begged me to come out as soon as possible. I know him well enough to know that he wouldn't have pressed me if it weren't something really serious. He made me promise not to talk to anyone else in Jefferson before I saw him."

"How long do you expect to be gone?"

"I don't know. It depends on what I find."

Nancy had no more questions about Paul, or Bill's trip, but it was clear she didn't entirely condone the whole matter. Her unspoken concern was about how this unscheduled sojourn would interfere with his work. He was her top-earning author and she liked keeping him close.

Bill handed her a three-by-five index card on which he had written Paul's name and home phone number. "In case you need to reach me and my cell's not working. I also sent it to you in an e-mail."

Their salads came; during the lull in the conversation Bill studied Nancy, thinking how little he really knew about her. She had a compact little body that looked 20 years younger than her face, which was heavily wrinkled from too much sun. He knew she was forty-six—too old for the little bows she often wore in her frosted hair, he thought. Then he remembered how much he owed her and flushed with guilt.

Later, over coffee, talk turned to the novel he'd recently finished and the publicity tour Nancy and his publisher were putting together for him. But that was months away.

When the waiter brought the check, Nancy studied it like a corporate proxy statement before plunking down her platinum American Express card. Bill was constantly amazed at the habits of the rich.

He shifted on his motel pillow.

Memories of Paul Watson began to surface. Before he left New York, Bill had looked through his high school senior yearbook for the first time in years. There were several pictures of Paul and him together. On the school newspaper. In a drama club production of *Hamlet*. Clowning around at a pep rally. Paul's lopsided grin, shaggy blond hair and blue eyes. Bill's studied seriousness and slicked-back brown hair. It was painful to see himself so young and thin, and innocent. They had graduated from Jefferson High thirty-two years ago next month.

Bill and Paul became friends in the fifth grade, just after Bill's family moved to a farm they bought near Jefferson. They were Kentucky tenant farmers who had finally saved enough money for a down payment on 40 acres of land across the Ohio River in Southern Indiana. They moved in the spring.

Bill's father built their house with his own hands that summer, working on it mostly at night so he could spend days tending the farm and its corn, soybeans, and valuable tobacco base. Until the house was finished, Bill and his parents lived in a rented trailer they pulled behind their pickup truck from town to the farm. They moved into the house in the fall; in December, Bill's brother, Ron, was born. By then Bill and Paul had become fast friends—more like brothers, really.

So, he was going to Indiana because Paul Watson was his friend and needed help.

For that alone, Bill would have gone. But there were other reasons that drew him west. Paul's plea had come in late April, about two months after Bill finished one book and was floundering around, trying to get started on another. He was at loose ends: bored, vaguely dissatisfied, and feeling a bit sorry for himself. A bad combination. He knew he needed a change. A jolt. The Vietnam trip hadn't done it. He needed to get involved in someone else's problems. Especially after living alone for more than two years.

A decade earlier Bill had left the newspaper business, after twenty years and some good reporting jobs, to freelance. His last job had been with The New York Times, where he covered national politics from the paper's Washington bureau on I Street. Most of his friends and colleagues thought he was crazy to leave a dream job. But top editors at the Times assured him he could return if things didn't work out. There were some false starts, and then he had written two moderately successful true crime books, one about a serial killer and another about a cult of neo-Nazis. Both had resulted in death threats against him that left him so depressed he vowed never to write in that genre again. He decided to write a book that was part politics and part travel; he spent the next two years traveling around Mexico and Central and South America with Jane. Then, after Nancy Luke wrangled a bigger advance than he had dared even hope for, he spent another year writing *Points South*. The hardback version was on the New York Times best-seller list for almost a year. The advance, the hardback royalties, and the paperback rights brought in more money than he had made in twenty years as a reporter. The next book, the one he had recently finished when Paul called, was a semi-autobiographical coming-of-age novel called *Look Down*. It was the only fiction Bill had ever written and was tough going. Since finishing the novel, he had been toying with the idea of another political and travel book, this time about the Middle East, where he had spent two years on assignment for the Houston Chronicle. But he couldn't get a handle on exactly where he wanted to go with the book. He didn't have a working title, which was his own personal warning flag that he hadn't thought it through. He probably would fly to Cairo or Amman and start traveling and talking to people and hope something would come into focus. That was how he'd started *Points South*, and he guessed it would work again. He was a strong reporter and interviewer partly because of his ability to blend in, to become almost invisible. "Non-threatening, until they read what he writes," an editor once said of him. Brown hair, brown eyes, medium build, regular features. Everyman with a reporter's notebook.

He began writing *Look Down* two Decembers ago, on a cold night between Christmas and New Year's Day after he returned home from a memorial service for Jane. They'd been married twenty-six years. Bill was almost forty-eight, and he didn't know how to grieve—only write. In the end, he discovered that for him they were the same. Jane had flown to Paris early in December to visit friends and was returning to New York on an Air France flight that was blown out of the sky over Newfoundland. Her only crime was buying an airplane ticket. He wrote and rewrote, and rewrote again, and dedicated the novel to her memory. Learning to grieve was a hard, word-by-word process. And then he had to learn how to stop. He had not really grieved when his mother and father died twelve years ago, within six months of each other. He had drifted apart from them; they were both in their late seventies, and their deaths were the natural consequence of a hard life. His younger brother, with whom he was never close, was killed in a prison fight seven years ago in Huntsville, Texas, where he was serving a life sentence for killing a deputy sheriff in a drunken brawl. Bill hadn't seen Ron for twenty years and felt like he was attending the funeral of a stranger. Ron's death left him with no family except some distant cousins in Kentucky he had only known as a child.

He was unable to be objective about whether *Look Down* was good or not. It would be out in the fall; Nancy told him it was headed for star treatment by The New York Times book review section and then to the best-seller list. She also said she was talking to some Hollywood people about a movie deal.

When Paul called, Bill was living in an empty space between *Look Down* and whatever was coming next. Since *Points South*, money hadn't been a problem. Jane used to say it was that book that gave them their fuck-you fund: enough money so that they didn't have to do anything they didn't want to, ever again.

Her life insurance and the settlement with Air France had increased that fund considerably.

Bill's reverie was broken by the telephone's ring. He picked up the receiver, wondering who would be calling him at this hour. No one knew exactly where he was.

"Hello."

"Good morning, Mr. Sanders. This is the front desk. It's six a.m."

"Oh, thanks. What time can I get breakfast?"

"Our coffee shop opens at six-thirty."

"Okay, thanks."

"You're welcome. Have a nice day."

Bill thought of several obscene responses as he hung up the phone. *When did a law get passed in America that everyone has to say have a nice goddamn day?* He liked living in countries where he couldn't understand the language and didn't have to be subjected to such inanities. *But what the hell? I probably will have a nice day.*

Sunday morning traffic was even lighter than Saturday. In a couple of hours, near Cincinnati, Bill pulled off at a rest stop to study a map. He liked maps. He had declined to rent a GPS along with the car. One of the things he liked about the Midwest was that he was never confused about directions: most property lines and fences run north-south or east-west. He decided to leave the interstate system at the border between Ohio and Indiana and take the scenic route to Jefferson, a state road running along the Ohio River and through the little river towns of Rising Sun, Patriot, Florence, and past the Markland Dam to Vevay and then on to Jefferson. Paul didn't expect him until that evening; he had time to spare.

Bill had telephoned Paul from New York Thursday night. Paul's voice was subdued, thick from alcohol, but he was much less panicky than when he had first called on Tuesday. He gave Bill directions to his new house in the country about ten miles west of Jefferson. Bill tried to get Paul to talk about whatever was troubling him, but his friend again refused to discuss it.

"It's too complicated. I can't talk about it on the phone. I'll tell you everything when you get here."

Then, his voice dropped almost to a whisper.

"I don't have many friends left. I'm afraid. You're the only person who can help me. Don't talk to anyone about this or try to find out anything until you've talked to me first. Please promise me this."

Bill promised.

He started to ask about Sharon but decided not to. He had last seen them, briefly, ten years ago in New York when he was just starting to freelance. They were headed to Europe for a vacation to celebrate Sharon's pregnancy, which came after years of trying and being told by doctors that she could never have children. Despite her age, almost forty, their daughter, Cindy, was born without a hitch. She favored Paul, lanky and blonde. Paul and Sharon were married while both were in college; Bill was Paul's best man at the Methodist church wedding in Indianapolis, Sharon's hometown. Bill would never forget the contrast Paul and Sharon projected when they were together: she, short and a bit chubby with dark bobbed hair; he, six feet tall, fair and slim.

Soon, Bill was following the Ohio River as it flowed southwest toward Jefferson. Spring was in full bloom; he turned off the car's air conditioner and opened the windows once he left the noise of the interstate. He could occasionally catch a whiff of honeysuckle as the air, cooled by the river, blew in his face. He hadn't been on this road for more than twenty-five years, but he remembered every twist and turn.

As he approached Florence, traffic picked up near the casino that had opened several years ago. To Bill, it looked garish and bizarrely out of place. He recalled reading a short item in the Times that plans for a similar casino in Jefferson had been voted down in a county election. But not in this county, where the economy was weaker, and every job and dollar counted.

As he drove past Markland Dam, he recalled the time he spent a week there as a young reporter for The Louisville Courier-Journal, filing daily stories about efforts to free a barge loaded with chlorine that had crashed into the locks. That had also been in the spring. The small farms downriver from the locks looked exactly as he remembered them.

As he approached Vevay, more memories began to surface. Locals called the town Vee-vee. It wasn't until he was a freshman in college that Bill learned the correct pronunciation, and spelling, of Vevay's Swiss namesake. He also remembered that when he and Paul were seniors at Jefferson High, they used to drive to Vevay and pay the town drunk to buy them beer at Vevay Liquors. Paul was always bolder and more adventurous than Bill in those days, but after they went to college they seemed to reverse roles. Paul returned to Jefferson as a guidance counselor; Bill took off, determined to see and do everything. He had been back to Jefferson only three times since graduating from Indiana University. Once to bury his mother and six months later to bury his father. Then seven years later to bury Ron. He had missed all his high school reunions, partly because he was halfway around the world or busy covering a story. But the main reason was that he never felt anything pulling him back to Jefferson—until now.

As Bill drove into Vevay's east side and on toward the town square, he wondered how many people lived there. A couple of thousand, maybe. Up ahead was the Vevay Hotel, covered in vines and sporting a freshly painted white sign advertising Sunday lunch. Bill pulled into the gravel parking lot, hoping he wasn't too late. A big clock in front of the hotel showed two o'clock.

The woman at the front desk told him there was plenty of time, that lunch was served on Sunday until three. She showed him into a bright dining room with a view of the river. The room was almost empty. Two couples were finishing their lunch at the far end. He took a seat near the window and studied the menu between glances at a coal-laden barge, low in the water, churning upstream.

"Bill Sanders?"

Bill looked up at a waitress who had approached his table. He was puzzled that she knew his name.

"Aren't you Bill Sanders?"

"I am. I'm sorry, but do I know you?"

"Bill, don't you remember? I'm Donna Sharp. Actually, now I'm Donna Wolfe. We were lab partners in Mr. Dennison's chemistry class."

Bill flushed with embarrassment. He did remember Donna Sharp, but that memory had little in common with the woman standing before him now. Donna Sharp was a cute, peppy cheerleader he had once wanted to date but never worked up the courage to ask out because she was so popular. Donna Wolfe was a stout woman whose gray hair was coiled into a bun on top of her head. She looked older than he knew she was; she reminded him of a storybook grandmother.

"What in the world brings you back to these parts? Where do you live now? Have you been to Jefferson?"

"Actually, I'm on my way there."

"Gosh, it must be great to travel around the way you do. You know, the Jefferson library had a display of your books last year. They also had a lot of old pictures of you, from high school and all. I'm real sorry about your wife. That was terrible. There was a story in The Jefferson Courier about her being on that plane. That story was also part of the display. I really am sorry."

"Thanks. I appreciate it."

"Are you gonna see Paul? Wasn't it terrible, what happened to him and his wife? What's her name? Sharon? Yeah, Sharon."

"What happened? I haven't heard."

"Gosh, it's been all in the news around here. Newspapers and television. TV trucks from Louisville and Indianapolis and Cincinnati with those big antennas that shoot up into the air were parked all over Jefferson. There was even a short item on CNN about it. But they all left after two or three days. You know how they are with a story like that. Big deal for a couple of days and then nothing. On to something else, I guess. Some of the online comments were awfully hateful to Paul. You really haven't heard?"

Bill shook his head. "I've been out of the country for the past month. In some remote places. I didn't get much news."

"Well, about two weeks ago their little girl disappeared. Some people think she ran away from home, but she's only ten. The police say they're investigating the possibility she was kidnapped."

Bill was stunned. Why hadn't Paul told him? Why all the secrecy? Why hadn't somebody called him? Then he realized that the only person from Jefferson he'd kept in contact with even remotely was Paul. Whatever national news the story of Cindy's disappearance made, he had missed it.

Donna continued, "When you see Paul, tell him I said hi and that I'm real sorry. I don't get back to Jefferson much these days, even though it's only twenty miles away. I guess you didn't know that I married Brent Wolfe. He's from Vevay. He has a real estate agency here that his father left him. Business isn't great, but we get along. Things picked up some with the casino, but not like we hoped. Bet you also didn't know that I have three boys and six grandchildren? Do you have any children?"

Bill again shook his head.

"Well, to each his own, I always say. Gosh, it's getting late. Do you want to order now?"

Bill ordered a chicken sandwich and a glass of iced tea. He only finished half the sandwich.

As he left, Donna introduced him to the hotel manager who escorted him to his car. "Come back anytime, Mr. Sanders. It's a pleasure to meet you. We don't get many famous authors around here."

Bill smiled to himself. *Guy's a natural at public relations.*

CHAPTER 2

Fifty feet underground in Ulster County, New York, Colonel Richard West studied a computer printout. He stood in the middle of a big, brightly lighted, white room. Against one wall was a bank of four computer monitors, a white-jacketed technician quietly working at each one. Another wall was lined with soundproof printers, constantly burping out sheets of numbers and text. Another wall contained a bank of color-coded phones.

Colonel West, a short man dressed in a dark three-piece business suit and a bright red tie, leaned heavily on his cane as he walked over to the fourth wall, covered with a huge map of the United States.

He located Indianapolis and ran his index finger south along Interstate 65 and then east a bit to Jefferson.

He looked again at the printout, pulled a red pushpin from his jacket pocket and stuck it between "Jeff" and "erson." There were five other red pins in Indiana. Stepping back a few feet, Colonel West studied the map, his eyes taking in hundreds of pins scattered around the country, many of them in tight clusters.

Still leaning on his cane, he walked over to a green phone and picked up the receiver and spoke quietly into the mouthpiece: "Sector nine. Case 85-43. Terminate. Acknowledge and report."

CHAPTER 3

Bill arrived in Jefferson with time to kill. He was bewildered at what Donna had told him. He thought about stopping at some fast-food restaurant with WiFi to check on the stories he had missed about Cindy's disappearance. He also considered stopping at The Jefferson Courier's office. Maybe a reporter could give him some background information that might be helpful. He finally decided to do neither. He wanted to talk to Paul first, which he had promised he would do. His encounter with Donna Wolfe had been an accident. A sudden memory reminded him that the newspaper office was probably closed on Sunday anyway. When he worked there it was an afternoon paper that published Monday through Saturday. He figured it still was. A quick drive past the office just off Main Street confirmed this.

He drove around town, amazed at how little things had changed. Whenever he described Jefferson to friends, he told them it was a town where Mark Twain could return and feel right at home. He realized again how true that was. The nineteenth-century buildings in the old part of town had been carefully preserved, partly out of civic pride and partly to attract bed-and-breakfast tourists looking for a calm weekend with a dose of nostalgia. Shopping malls, Walmarts, and new housing developments were kept on the outskirts of town. The population had remained a stable eight thousand or so over the years, mainly because of Jefferson's relative isolation, which also saved its Neo-Classical and Federal architecture from developments spawned by growing populations. The town was just far enough away from Cincinnati, Louisville, and Indianapolis so that it had never become a bedroom community for those cities. It existed on its own terms, supported mainly by farming, tourism, and some light manufacturing.

Bill parked in front of the high school, built a block from the riverfront in the nineteen-twenties, got out of the car and walked up to the building's massive wooden front doors. The smell of locker rooms and polished wood floors seeped from behind the locked doors, releasing a flood of memories from more than thirty years ago. His senior prom had been in the school's gym. He could still smell Patti Smith's too-strong lavender perfume. They kept in touch for a year or so after high school. Bill had no idea where she was now, other than in his memory, dancing at the prom. Other smells flooded his memory. Burning leaves in the fall, their acrid yet somehow pleasant odor mingled with the pungent, ripe-apple smell of cured tobacco hanging in warehouses that used to ring the town.

He walked over to Main Street and strolled through the historic business district. The buildings and stores were much the same, although some names were different. Taylor's Drug Store was still there. The Jefferson Theater now had two screens, according to the marquee. The Douglas Sandwich Shop was now called The Jefferson Cafe and its interior had been remodeled. Wong Hardware. Cosby Men's Wear. Buy-Rite Furniture. Weisman's Jewelers. Humes Department Store. All the same. Probably run by sons and daughters of the people who ran the stores when Bill was a student.

The only place open on Main Street was Hink's Hamburger Heaven, a popular hangout when he was in high school. It was still open twenty-four hours a day and hadn't changed a bit; the same bulbs seemed to be missing from the blinking neon sign. The familiar smell of frying meat and onions wafted a block in either direction. He went in, straddled a chrome counter stool and ordered two hamburgers and a milkshake. He felt like The Ghost of Jefferson Past.

It was after five when he returned to the car and headed to Paul's house, following the detailed directions Paul had given him.

Twenty minutes later, he wound the car down a gravel road and into Paul's front yard. The house, a big, two-story log cabin, sat in an isolated clearing deep in a stand of woods. There were no other houses within at least a quarter mile.

The house was closed up, despite the warm weather. A red Jeep Wrangler was parked next to the front porch. Bill honked his car's horn before getting out and walking to the main door.

He rang the doorbell, listening to its echoes inside the house. No sign of anyone home. He knocked loudly on the wooden door. Nothing.

He turned the doorknob and the door swung open, revealing a large rustic living room and a massive stone fireplace. Paul, disheveled and snoring quietly, was sprawled face up on the sofa with his left leg and arm hanging to the floor. The stuffy, demi-dark room reeked of charred wood and liquor. A half-empty bottle of Wild Turkey sat on the floor next to an overturned empty glass.

Bill walked over to the sofa and looked down at Paul, startled at what he saw. It was not just that Paul was drunk. His face, always light-skinned and smooth, had a gray cast and was covered with heavy, wrinkled lines that gave him a tortured look. He was much thinner than usual; his clothes hung loosely on his body.

Bill lifted Paul's feet and adjusted his body so that he was full-length on the sofa. He picked up the liquor bottle and glass and took them to the kitchen. The sink was full of dirty dishes and the table was piled high with unopened mail and newspapers.

Bill went upstairs and found what he assumed was Paul and Sharon's bedroom. He took a pillow off the bed, found a blanket in a closet and carried them downstairs. He put the pillow under Paul's head and covered the bottom half of his body with the blanket. Paul didn't stir. Bill checked his friend's pulse and decided he was okay, just passed out.

Bill went out to his car and brought in his duffel bag and backpack. He found what appeared to be a guest room next to the kitchen. He took his laptop out of the backpack, placed it on the bedside table and plugged in its charger. He stared at the computer's pulsating light for a few seconds and then lay down on the bed for a few minutes to think. He wished he had come directly here instead of poking around town. He might have stopped Paul before he drank too much. He wondered where Sharon was. And what about Cindy? Was she still missing? Had Paul learned some awful news? He thought about going out and shaking him awake but decided to let him sleep it off.

A little later Bill went outside and looked around the house, bathed now in deep evening shade from massive trees around the clearing. The house was eerily isolated, not visible from any road. No other houses were within sight. Birds rustled in trees and bushes. Two squirrels raced across the recently mowed clearing. Bill felt mildly depressed, wondering if he was doing the right thing.

He went back into the house. Paul hadn't stirred. Bill went to the kitchen, found a clean glass and poured himself a stiff drink from the Wild Turkey bottle. He went back into the guest room, closed the door and lay on the bed without undressing. In a few minutes, he was asleep.

A crash awoke him. The room was pitch black.

"Bill? Is that you, Bill?"

"I'm here, Paul. In the bedroom." Bill fumbled to find the bedside light and flicked it on. He glanced at his watch. Three o'clock.

Another crash. Bill jumped off the bed and opened the door leading out to the main room. The only light was the faint glow from his bedside. Paul stood awkwardly by the sofa. An end table was on its side.

Paul turned and switched on a floor lamp by the fireplace. In the harsh light he looked even more haggard than before.

Bill walked over to Paul and the two embraced. Tears welled up in Paul's eyes. "God, I'm glad to see you. I'm glad you're here."

"We need to talk, Paul. How do you feel? You want to go back to sleep and talk in the morning? Or later in the morning, I should say."

"No, let's talk now. I'm okay, I guess. Help me make some coffee and straighten up in here."

CHAPTER 4

By the time they had made coffee and built a fire against the early morning chill, it was after four. Bill scrambled some eggs for himself. Paul, understandably, didn't want anything to eat.

Paul settled back on the sofa; Bill sat in a club chair next to the stone fireplace. The chair faced the sofa at an angle. Bill studied Paul's face. His blue eyes were red-rimmed and swollen; his hand trembled as he sipped the hot, black coffee from a mug.

"So," Bill said. "Let's talk."

"You're gonna think I'm crazy. Maybe I am."

"Well, just tell me. I know about Cindy. I ran into Donna Sharp in Vevay and she told me. Why didn't you tell me? Why the secrecy? Especially if everybody else around here knows. Donna said it's been in the news."

"I wanted you to get the story from me. Unfiltered. Especially after I first called you and realized you didn't know anything about it."

"Where's Sharon?"

"She's gone. Left. She went to her parents in Indianapolis."

"Why? Why would she leave with Cindy missing? She still is missing?"

"Yes." Paul's eyes began to well up. "Let me try to start at the beginning. The story's been all over the news, even a bit on CNN. Thank God, the story died quickly. At least on the national level. But they only had part of the story. The Sheriff—Dave Taylor. Remember him? He was a year behind us in school. He and Sharon are the only ones who know the whole story. So far, Dave's kept a lid on it. Mainly out of friendship for me. But I'm not sure how long that's gonna last."

Bill didn't like the ominous turn this was taking.

"Paul, start over. Tell me from the beginning."

"Okay. First, here's the official story that's been in the news. Two weeks ago Friday I came home late. Sharon was asleep, and Cindy was missing from her bed. The house was locked from the inside and there was no sign of forced entry. Cindy was simply gone. I woke Sharon and we searched everywhere before calling the Sheriff's office. Over two weeks have passed and there has been absolutely no sign of her or what may have happened to her. The woods and fields have been searched for miles around here. Her picture has been all over. Nothing. Some people think she ran away. Some think she was somehow lured out of the house and kidnapped."

"What do you think?"

"I know."

Bill was shocked by Paul's answer. "What the hell do you mean you know?"

"I mean I know. But Dave and Sharon don't believe me. They think I'm crazy. Sharon was nearly hysterical when her folks came down here and picked her up last week. But all they know is the official version. Sharon's too embarrassed to tell them what I told her and Dave, and she refuses to talk to me. We'd been having some problems before this happened ... she thought I was drinking too much. So, I called you. I had nowhere else to turn."

Faint fingers of light were beginning to streak the eastern sky.

"Paul, what happened to Cindy?"

"She was abducted by an unidentified flying object. A UFO."

CHAPTER 5

In the moments of silence that followed, Bill felt his body grow lighter. The room grew larger and the distance between Paul and him greater.

Bill flushed with anger and the room and his body returned to normal.

"Goddammit, Paul, what the fuck are you talking about? You call me all the way out here to tell me some science fiction fantasy? What kind of shit are you trying to pull?" By now Bill was shouting.

Paul suddenly began to sob and buried his face in both hands. Bill got up and went to the kitchen for some more coffee.

He returned to the living room and began to pace in front of Paul and the sofa. He didn't know whether to be angry or sad, or both.

Paul suddenly stood up and turned toward Bill. When he spoke, his voice was hard and cold.

"Listen, we've known each other nearly all our lives. Do you really think I would bring you out here to lie to you? Have we ever lied to each other? I know what I saw. And if you won't believe me, or at least hear me out, then I'm lost. I have nowhere to turn."

Bill's anger had cooled a bit. It was true. He and Paul had never bullshitted each other.

"I'm sorry, Paul. But you can understand my reaction. Sit down. Tell me what happened." *Or what you think happened.*

"That Friday night when I came home late—it was almost midnight—I had been drinking. But I swear I wasn't drunk. As

I started to turn down our lane, I noticed lights over the house. They seemed to pulsate, red and green and white. My first thought was that it was a helicopter, but there wasn't any noise.

"Then when I drove into the clearing, the whole house was bathed in light. It was like a movie crew had set up lights around the house. When my eyes adjusted a little to the brightness, I looked up and that's when I saw it. A big goddamn machine shaped like a triangle, bigger than the house and the clearing, was just hanging there in the sky about a hundred feet over the roof. Again, I thought it must be a helicopter, but it was too big and there was still no sound. It was absolutely silent.

"I was scared shitless. I jumped out of the car and started to run toward the front door, screaming for Sharon. Before I could get five steps, I was hit by some kind of electricity. I fell on my back unable to move or make a sound. But I could still see the machine and the east side of the house, where Cindy's room is upstairs. Then I noticed a blue beam of light about two feet wide running from the machine, or whatever in the hell it was, to Cindy's window. Cindy was floating inside that beam of blue light, in the air, between her window and the object. I could see her clearly. She was asleep in her green pajamas, her arms at her side.

"I must have passed out, because when I awoke about fifteen or twenty minutes later everything appeared normal. I was lying on my back in the clearing. No machine. No lights. I could move, although I felt stiff and sick to my stomach, and dazed. It was about twenty minutes past midnight.

"I ran into the house screaming for Cindy and Sharon. Cindy's bed was empty, and Sharon was sound asleep. But she was sleeping like she was drugged. I had a hard time waking her up and when she did get up, she was confused and groggy. There was a funny smell in the house, kind of like burned cinnamon, but it was gone in a few minutes. We searched the house and yard. We even looked into the edge of the woods and out on the road before we called Dave's office. He and his deputies also searched the house and the yard, as well as the woods.

"When I told Sharon, and later Dave, what I had seen, their reactions were like yours—only worse. I had liquor on my breath and they both accused me of being drunk and imagining the whole thing. Nobody in this area reported anything strange that night. I think for a time Dave suspected me of having something to do with Cindy's disappearance. But I was with some teachers from the school until right before I drove home, and Sharon said she had looked in on Cindy at about eleven-thirty. I've agreed to take a lie detector test this week, but Dave said they're not always reliable.

"I've lost my daughter and my wife. I'm telling you what I saw. I say it was a UFO because I don't know what else to call it." His voice dropped. "Please help me."

The dark shadows around the house began to retreat in the face of the early morning sun. The fire had burned down to a pile of glowing embers.

Bill looked at Paul and then at his cup of coffee, now cold.

"Do you need to call the school and tell them you won't be in today?"

"No. I'm on a leave of absence until this is cleared up one way or the other."

"Do you need money?"

"No. They were very nice. They're still paying me."

Sunlight was slanting through the kitchen window.

"Bill?"

"Yes?"

"There are two things I haven't told you. Or anyone else."

"What are they?"

"When Cindy was in that blue light, she wasn't being pulled from her window. She was floating *toward* the window. And just before I passed out, I heard something in the distance: the heavy thumping sound of a helicopter."

It took Bill a few seconds for Paul's revelation to sink in. Suddenly, nothing seemed to make sense.

"I don't understand. If she was floating toward the house ... the window ... why wasn't she there when you finally came to and went into the house?"

Paul started to tear up again but checked himself.

"I don't know. I'm just telling you what I saw. I know it sounds crazy. Maybe I am crazy."

Things aren't fitting together here. Or else there are some missing pieces. If the UFO was returning Cindy to her room, where was she when Paul ran into the house a few minutes later? And what about the helicopter he said he heard? Did he mistake a helicopter for a UFO, which seems likely? But what the hell was a helicopter doing out here in the middle of the night? Was the beam of blue light simply a reflection off a cable or something? But why would someone in a helicopter be abducting, or returning, Cindy?

CHAPTER 6

Bill unpacked his duffel and then shaved and showered. Paul, worn out, slept on the sofa. Bill booted up his laptop to check his e-mail, but there was no WiFi signal. He was pretty sure Paul had a computer, but apparently not WiFi. He would check with him later.

Bill left a note on the kitchen table saying that he had gone into town and would return in the middle of the afternoon. He suggested they go out for dinner that evening. Paul had given him a house key, which Bill stuck in his wallet.

He wanted to look at some recent back issues of The Jefferson Courier at the newspaper's office and he wanted to talk to Dave Taylor. He also wanted to be alone for a while to think. Or to try to figure out what to think. He had always dismissed unidentified flying objects as part of some kook fringe. But now he had a trusted friend telling him he had not only seen one, but that it was somehow involved in the disappearance of his daughter.

At the Courier office Bill was delighted to find that Graham Neal, the man who had hired him to cover basketball games while he was in high school and later hired him as a reporter during the summers between his college years, was still the editor. Not surprising, since his family had owned the newspaper for almost a century. The old man roared with joy when Bill stuck his head into his small office. Neal was older and grayer but had the same firm handshake and springy walk.

"Son of a bitch! Where the hell have you been? Last time I heard you were in South America. Damn, it's good to see you again!"

Neal, which was all anyone could ever remember calling him, insisted on showing Bill around the office, which had been remodeled five years ago. Only a couple of office workers had been there long enough to remember him.

"You know how it is," Neal said. "We hire young reporters and editors, train them and then they go off and get jobs on bigger papers. Just like you did. But you switched to books. Guess you hit the jackpot, huh?"

"Yeah, I guess I've done okay."

"I was mighty sorry to hear about your wife."

"Thanks. It's taken awhile, but I'm dealing with it."

"So, what brings you to Jefferson?"

"Well, I came to help Paul and Sharon Watson."

"That's right. I forgot. You and Paul were best friends. Sad story. I wonder if they'll ever find that little girl."

"I sure hope so. Neal, can I look at some back issues of the paper? I didn't know anything about what happened to Cindy until yesterday, and I want to catch up on the details. I know the stories are online, but I'd like to see the actual papers. There's no context to a single story online. Plus, I guess I'm a little old-fashioned."

"Sure. Help yourself. But there's not much. She seems to have vanished into thin air. You know, there are rumors around town that the Sheriff's office might be withholding some facts in the case. Dave Taylor swears not. Our new reporter, Daniel Scott's his name, has been digging around, but I don't think he's found anything. If you hear something, let me know. You always were the best reporter we ever had here, even if you were only a part-timer. Remember when you had the whole damned city council pissed off at you and the paper? The bastards tried to organize an advertising boycott, but it never got anywhere."

Bill remembered. He had written a story exposing a sweetheart deal between the council members and Jefferson's major merchants. The politicians, Democrats and Republicans, were getting all kinds of freebies ranging from things as petty as movie tickets to clothes and groceries and even the use of new cars, which were later sold by dealers as demonstrators. In return, the merchants could count on favorable treatment on tax and zoning issues. Two council members resigned and there were a lot of red faces on Main Street, but not much else came of it. The county attorney refused to take the case to a grand jury, and the story just petered out after Bill returned to Indiana University for his senior year. That was his last summer at the Courier. After graduation he got a reporting job with The Louisville Courier-Journal. Within a year he was transferred to the paper's Washington bureau.

"Say," Neal continued, "how about we do an interview with you? Famous writer returns to his hometown to help an old friend. I'll write it myself."

"Thanks, but I'd rather you didn't. I want to be able to poke around a bit without everybody knowing what I'm up to. Maybe later, when this is all over."

"Okay. Your call. But one thing you're not going to get out of is dinner at my house. Marge will be delighted to see you again."

"That'd be great. Give me a couple of days to get my bearings. I trust you still know how to make a martini?"

"Now you're talking."

Neal offered Bill a desk to use and in a few minutes Sarah Wong, the office manager who had worked at the Courier when he was a young reporter, brought a stack of papers spanning the last month.

It didn't take long to see that Neal was right. There wasn't much. Lots of photographs of Cindy and Paul and Sharon. The usual stories, all by Daniel Scott, and pictures about the search parties that had combed the countryside. That was about it. The quotes from Dave Taylor didn't give a hint that there was anything more to the story than there appeared to be. Nothing of what Paul had told Bill earlier that morning. The most recent article reported that Sharon's father had offered a twenty-thousand-dollar reward for information leading to Cindy, alive or dead.

But something else caught Bill's eye. It was a box below

the fold on the front page of an issue that was dated exactly one week prior to Cindy's disappearance. It briefly recounted the story of two teenage boys who were picked up near the river by the police at one o'clock in the morning. They were charged with possession of marijuana and released to their parents. But before their parents came to the police station to pick the two up, the boys told officers they had seen a UFO just before midnight, hovering over the Ohio River near Jefferson's waterfront.

They described it as triangular-shaped, and bigger than a barn.

CHAPTER 7

It was almost eleven when Dave left the Courier office and walked four blocks along Main Street to the Madison County courthouse. The Sheriff's office was off to the side of the building, the double-door entrance beneath a big sign reading: David G. Taylor, Sheriff, Madison County, Indiana. Opposite the entrance were three brown and tan police cruisers.

As Bill started toward the doors, Dave Taylor pushed through them, squinted at the sun and reached for a pair of sunglasses in his shirt pocket. He had put on extra weight over the years and his hair was nearly all gray, but he was instantly recognizable to Bill.

"Dave?"

"I'm Sheriff Dave Taylor. Can I help you?"

"You don't recognize me, do you?"

"No, I reckon I don't."

"I'm Bill Sanders. I was a year ahead of you in high school."

"Bill Sanders! Son of a gun. What brings you back to these parts? You're pretty famous. Say, I was sorry to hear about your wife."

"Thanks. Can we go somewhere and talk privately for a few minutes?"

"Sure. Let's walk over to the Jefferson Cafe. I've practically got my own private booth there. It used to be the Douglas Sandwich Shop. Remember?"

"Sure do. Spent many a happy hour there."

"Me, too. Mrs. Douglas has been dead I guess six, seven years now. Come on."

It was early for the usual lunch crowd; the restaurant was

nearly empty. Bill followed the Sheriff past the counter, and they took seats in a booth in the back.

A waitress brought coffee as soon as they sat down. She smiled at Dave. "Anything else, Sheriff?"

"That's it. Thanks, Darleen."

Dave blew the steam off his coffee and sipped it.

"So, what can I do for you?"

"It's about Paul Watson. I came back to Jefferson because he asked me to help him. I spent last night at his house. He told me the whole story."

"Oh, that's a tough one. What did he tell you?"

"Dave, he told me everything he told you and Sharon. We're the only three people who have heard his version of Cindy's disappearance. So please level with me. I'm trying to help him. What the hell is going on? Do you have any idea what happened?"

"Well, in my opinion there are two things going on here. One is that Cindy disappeared. I don't know how or why. Where does a ten-year-old girl go in the middle of the night? The second thing is I think Paul has gone around the bend. He needs psychiatric help. He's been drinking a lot lately. Did he tell you he was drunk the night Cindy disappeared? And now he's come up with this loony story about a UFO. Either he's crazy or he invented that story to cover up whatever family problems caused Cindy to run away, assuming she did."

Darleen refilled their coffee cups. Three men had come in while they were talking. They were sitting on stools at the counter near the front of the restaurant.

Bill poured some milk into his coffee.

"Dave, I agree it's a weird story. But I know Paul, and I just can't believe he would lie to me. Is it possible he saw something normal, a helicopter or an airplane, and thought it was a UFO? I saw a story in the Courier about two kids who claimed they saw a UFO down by the river a week before Cindy disappeared. Could there be a connection?"

"Come on, Bill. Get real. Those kids had been smoking pot. Hell, they could have seen a purple elephant. Paul probably read the story and got the idea in his head. If you want to help Paul, forget this UFO shit and get him some professional help. You know, I suspected at first that he had something to do with Cindy's disappearance. But he was drinking with some teachers that night. I checked it out. And Sharon said she saw Cindy about eleven-thirty. I guess he's in the clear on that score. Did he tell you the doors to his house were all locked? She had to have run away. Not much else fits."

"But why would she run away? Where would she run away to?"

"Who the hell knows. She's ten years old. Paul's drinking too much. Maybe he and Sharon had been fighting a lot and Cindy was upset."

"What about Sharon? Did you suspect her at all?"

"Yeah, at first. You always suspect the parents in cases like this. But a neighbor who was taking a walk said she saw Sharon and Cindy pull into their driveway about six that night. Sharon said Cindy was in bed later that night. I believed her."

"Could she have been abducted? By someone in a conventional way, I mean."

"By a locksmith, maybe. Remember, the house was locked."

"What if she ran away and got picked up by somebody later?"

"Very possible. But we put out every kind of alert we could on her. We simply have nothing to go on. No witnesses. No vehicle."

"Paul said he was going to take a lie detector test."

"Yeah, the State Police are going to give it to him later this week. But those things aren't foolproof. Why do you think they can't be admitted as evidence in court?"

"What about Sharon?"

"We could arrange one when she comes back from Indianapolis. But she's not the one with the tall tale."

Bill sighed. He was more confused than ever.

"Well, thanks anyway," he said. "Listen, will you keep me filled in on anything you learn? I promise to keep anything you tell me to myself. I won't even tell Paul, if you don't want me to."

"Yeah, sure. If you'll do the same for me."

"Absolutely. Here's a card with my cell phone number. Guess I can always reach you through your office."

"Sure can. How long are you gonna be in town?"

"I don't know. A couple of weeks, maybe. I'm staying at Paul's. I'll hang around until I'm satisfied there's nothing more I can do."

"Well, I got to get back to the office. Good to see you after all these years."

Dave stuck Bill's card in his shirt pocket, eased out of the booth, and walked toward the door. He stopped to chat briefly with one of the men who had come in earlier.

After Dave left, Bill had a third cup of coffee and a piece of rhubarb pie, remembering the days when Mrs. Douglas made pies every morning. He took a notebook out of his jacket and made some notes, mainly to give himself the sense he was doing something or getting somewhere.

He tried to pay for the coffee and pie, but Darleen wouldn't take his money.

"We don't charge the Sheriff. Guess we don't charge people who are with him either."

The lunch crowd was beginning to arrive as Bill stepped out onto Main Street into the bright spring sunlight.

CHAPTER 8

Bill decided to return to the Courier office, mainly because he couldn't think of anything else to do or anywhere else to go.

As he started to walk back down Main Street, he was bemused by how deserted the town looked. He knew this perception was the result of navigating crowded New York streets for too many years.

At the Courier, the receptionist said Neal had gone home for lunch a few minutes earlier. Sarah Wong waved at him from her desk across the small newsroom. He pushed through a low swinging gate and headed in her direction. Sarah was a Chinese-American whose family had lived in Jefferson for well over a century. Her ancestors came to the American Midwest in the 1860s to work on the railroads; some of them liked Jefferson and stayed on. By the 1920s, the Wongs owned a successful hardware store that was still going strong. Sarah's two children, her husband, and her brother all worked there; she had an independent streak and staked out her own career at the newspaper office. She knew everything about the Courier and kept it running smoothly. Neal often called her his most valuable employee.

"Neal still goes home for lunch with Marge?" Bill asked as he sat in a chair next to Sarah's desk. Neal and Marge had been childhood sweethearts who had gotten married right out of high school and been inseparable ever since.

"Yep," Sarah replied. "Same as always. What are you up to?"

"Just looking around. Trying to help Paul Watson."

"I know. Neal told me why you came after you left this morning. Everybody's real upset over that whole mess. Have you talked to Daniel Scott? He's been covering it. Still is."

"No, but I'd like to."

"I don't think he knows anything he hasn't put in his stories, but you never know. He'll be back later this afternoon."

"I'm going to the library for a while. Will he be here by around three?"

"I imagine. He's at the county agent's office working on a farming story. It's been a dry spring."

Bill paused, thinking about how his father used to worry about the weather and his crops. The years fell away as images of his family's life in Jefferson intruded into the present.

"That reminds me. I ought to drive out and visit my family's old farm."

"Well, brace yourself. It's a subdivision now."

"Oh, I didn't know." Past images gave way to a vague feeling of loneliness. "Well, nothing stays the same."

"Yep."

"Sarah, do you still keep clip files of local stories by subject? Or is everything online?"

"Both, sort of. The recent stuff goes online. We're still working on scanning in the older stories. But we also keep physical clips of recent stories. But it's a little hit and miss. Just like when you were here."

"Do you have a file on UFOs? I saw a story in a back issue that you gave me earlier about some boys who had reported seeing a UFO down by the river about a week before Paul's daughter disappeared. Have there been any other sightings like that around here?"

"Yep, lots. Over the last year. For a while it was all anybody talked about, but I guess people got tired of it. To tell you the truth, I think the whole thing just plain embarrassed a lot of folks. We've reported some of the sightings, although Neal was against it at first. He still isn't very happy about it. He thinks they're because of pranks or publicity hounds. Seems like most of the reports come from kids or drunks. They're mostly the ones prowling around at night. You want to see the stories? I could print them out for you. I think there were only about six cases that we reported, including the one you saw. They were the only ones Neal would agree to print. How come you're interested in them?"

"That would be great. But if there have been several reports and stories, why didn't the story I saw about the latest one say there had been others?"

"Neal. He said he didn't want to feed such silliness by reporting it as a trend. Some people from a big UFO organization came to town a couple of times, but I don't think anything came of it. The paper ignored them. Hold on and I'll find those stories and print them out for you."

"Thanks, Sarah."

Ten minutes later she handed him a file folder containing printouts of the stories.

"I'll look at these later. When Daniel Scott comes in, tell him I'll be back sometime between three and four."

"Sure. But you still haven't answered my question."

"What?"

"Why are you interested in these UFO stories?"

"I don't know. Just curiosity, I guess."

Halfway along the five-block walk to the library, Bill stopped to buy some chewing gum at Taylor's Drugs, which looked and smelled the same as when he was in high school. He had never felt so conflicted in his life. He was almost certain that whatever had in fact caused the sightings and the talk of the sightings was the source of Paul's "experience" the night Cindy disappeared. Maybe Dave Taylor was right, but why hadn't he mentioned all the other sightings? Maybe Paul had a stress- and alcohol-induced hallucination. Yet Bill couldn't forget his friend's haunted look. *Do you really think I would bring you out here to lie to you? Have we ever lied to each other? I know what I saw. And if you won't believe me, or at least hear me out, then*

I'm lost. I have nowhere to turn.

Bill did a double take when he reached the library. It was gone. Or at least the one he had worked in for a year in the ninth grade was gone, replaced by an imposing red brick structure that came right out to the sidewalk, covering the front yard he used to mow.

Inside, he didn't recognize anyone. Martha Pixon, the head librarian who had hired him, must be long dead. It had been a well-kept library secret that she used to consign to the big coal-fired furnace in the basement any books she considered too risqué for Jefferson. It was an even better-kept secret that Bill used to steal lunch money from the change box for overdue fines.

Bill settled into a comfortable chair in the reading room and began to read the six stories Sarah had given him. Five minutes later he was finished. They were all short and pretty much alike. None had bylines. Reports of strange lights in the sky. Three accounts of people who said they saw actual craft, all big and triangular-shaped. Like what Paul described. Bill was puzzled by this. He had always assumed flying saucers were round.

He put the clips back into the file folder and turned to recent issues of The New York Times, The Washington Post, and The Wall Street Journal to catch up on the news. Nancy Luke was quoted in a book column in the Times on the future of fiction. He made a mental note to give her a call in a couple of days.

Thirty minutes later, Bill, feeling a bit restless, wandered around the stacks. In the children's section was a large bulletin board. The six UFO stories he had just read were thumbtacked on the board, surrounded by construction paper cutouts of flying saucers and bug-eyed aliens.

On his way out, Bill noticed a fishbowl with a sign in front asking for donations to help the library buy new books. He dropped in two twenty-dollar bills.

*

"Is Daniel Scott back yet?" Bill asked Sarah as he walked back into the Courier newsroom.

"Not yet, but he should be any minute. Neal called and left a message for you. He said he's not feeling well and probably won't be in until tomorrow morning. He wants you to come to dinner at six on Wednesday."

"Tell him that's fine. I'll see him then."

Bill waited another fifteen minutes. Still no Daniel.

Another quarter hour went by, and Bill decided he had better check on Paul.

Sarah was on the phone, but she put her hand over the receiver when Bill approached her desk, indicating he could interrupt.

"Tell Daniel I'll catch him later. Maybe tomorrow."

Sarah nodded that she understood. Bill scribbled Paul's name and phone number on a piece of paper and handed it to Sarah, along with a business card containing his cell phone number. "In case you need to reach me," he whispered. She nodded again.

It was almost four when Bill left the Courier and began the drive back to Paul's house.

Paul was still asleep on the sofa. There were no signs that he'd had anything more to drink.

Bill kicked his shoes off and lay down on the guest bed. He pulled his cell phone out of his pants pocket and put it next to his laptop on the bedside table. The next thing he knew Paul was shaking his shoulder.

"I just saw your note. Do you still want to get some dinner?"

"Yeah. What time is it?"

"Almost seven."

After Bill had splashed some water on his face and changed shirts, he realized that he was ravenous.

"I'm really hungry. Anyplace around here to get a good steak?"

"New place about a mile from here. The Cattle Guard. It's pretty good."

"Let's do it."

"Do you mind driving? I'm still a little shaky from all that Wild Turkey last night."

Except for Paul's directions, they hardly spoke on the way to the restaurant.

Once inside, amid the wall-mounted steer horns and photographs of cowboy movie stars, they were seated in a booth near the bar. Since it was Monday night, the place was only about half full. A waitress named Sandy, who was dressed like a cowgirl, took their orders. Bill ordered a vodka martini and a New York strip sirloin. Paul ordered coffee and an omelet.

"What'd you do today?" Paul asked.

"Well, I stopped at the Courier and saw Neal and then I talked to Dave Taylor."

"Dave thinks I'm nuts, doesn't he?"

"Well, that not exactly how he put it. But I guess that about sums it up. When are you supposed to take the lie detector test?"

"As soon as Dave arranges it with the State Police. Probably Thursday or Friday."

Sandy brought the coffee and martini. Bill sipped the drink slowly, not expecting much. To his surprise, it was perfect.

"Hope this doesn't bother you," he said, pointing to the martini.

"Not as long as I don't have to drink it."

Behind the bar, a glass crashed to the floor. Paul jumped. Bill noticed that his hands were trembling a bit as he sipped his coffee.

"Paul, tell me about the problems you and Sharon were having. You said she thought you were drinking too much?"

"Yeah. It all started about a year and a half ago. I began having these anxiety attacks. No, that's too mild. Panic attacks. I would be overcome with unreasonable fear and dread. I couldn't sleep because of nightmares. The only thing that helped was to drink. Sharon never understood that. She wanted me to go to a shrink, but I resisted. You know how it is in a small town. Especially if you're the high school guidance counselor."

His voice dropped to a soft whisper.

"Anyway, we fought over my drinking. I guess when Cindy disappeared it was the final straw for Sharon. Especially when she heard my account of what I saw. I can't blame her."

Suddenly, his voice turned hard and definite.

"But I know this. I wasn't drunk and I wasn't dreaming. I saw what I saw."

Bill shifted in his seat and took another sip of his martini.

"Okay. Let's say I believe you ...."

"You mean you really don't, but you'll pretend?"

"No. Just bear with me. Let's just explore several trails here. And don't be so damn touchy. I'm here, aren't I?"

"I'm sorry. Go ahead."

"Let's follow through on your story. You said it looked like Cindy was being put back into her room from the UFO. But earlier you had said a UFO abducted her. Then you said you heard the sound of a helicopter. What do you think was happening?"

"I don't know. I've gone over and over it in my mind. Maybe the angle of my vision made it only look like she was floating from the UFO to her room. Maybe it was the other way around. Or maybe she had been abducted and was being returned. Was the helicopter I heard just one that happened to be in the area, or was it somehow connected to what was going on? What the hell does a helicopter have to do with a UFO?"

If Cindy were being put back in her room, where the hell is she? Some things are STILL not hanging together here. But I can't press Paul too hard right now. He's too fragile.

"Another thing. Sharon is a light sleeper. Yet she slept through all this and when I finally got her awake it was as though she had been drugged. I'm thinking, what the fuck is going on ...."

Sandy appeared with their food. She pretended not to notice that Paul had begun to cry.

They finished the meal in silence. Bill, who had been ravenous, ate all his steak and everything that came with it. Paul only picked around the edges of his omelet.

Later, Sandy brought coffee.

"Are you up to some more questions, or do you want to wait until tomorrow?" Bill asked.

"No, I'm okay. Sorry, but I just lose it every now and then."

"Hell, who wouldn't considering what you're going through."

"I guess."

"Paul, tell me something. Have you known about the rash of UFO sightings around here over the past year?"

"Sure. Who didn't? It caused a lot of excitement at school—some of the kids reported sightings—and there were some stories in the paper. Must have been stories in some out-of-town papers too, or maybe TV, because several people from a big UFO research group—I think it's called MUFON—showed up a couple of times, but I don't think anything ever came of it."

"Did you know that a week before Cindy disappeared that some kids who were smoking pot reported seeing a triangular-shaped UFO, like the one you described, down by the river? Dave Taylor thinks there's a connection, that their report may have planted a suggestion in your mind. That's not an unreasonable assumption, and we need to deal with it if I'm going to help you."

"I know. Jesus, I know. I've been over this a thousand times in my mind. I know what the kids reported. But I also know what I saw and heard. I didn't experience some projection or hallucination. How many times do I have to say it?"

"Okay, Paul. Here's the deal. I believe you. At least, I believe you saw something you can't explain. It's unidentified, but I'm not ready to believe it was a flying saucer—not yet. Whatever it was, it apparently had something to do with Cindy. Find out about it, find out about her. Maybe. At least, I hope. I don't know any other way to go. Let's get you pulled together and get busy. Tomorrow, let's start checking all the houses around your place for at least a mile and see if anybody saw anything that night. I know the police have probably asked all these people if they know anything about Cindy, but I bet they weren't asked if they saw or heard anything strange in the sky. This plan okay with you?"

"God Almighty, yes."

CHAPTER 9

Marine One banked as it approached the south lawn of the White House. The President glanced up from a briefing book he had been reading during the seventy-mile flight from Camp David. Through the frame of the helicopter's window he could see the lights of Washington as spring darkness settled over the city; the lights appeared to radiate from the executive mansion, like spokes of a giant wheel extending toward an invisible rim. The President focused on the scene below. No matter how jaded he had become about Washington, he never tired of this view of the White House.

With a gentle rocking motion, the helicopter settled onto the south lawn. The President yawned as he closed the briefing book and stuck it into a leather brief case, which was immediately scooped up by a military aide sitting in the seat next to the President. Four Secret Service agents sitting behind the president were on their feet as the helicopter ramp was lowered. The President eased his bulk out of his seat, waved at the two pilots and stepped out into the cool spring night. There were two more Secret Service agents there to greet him; otherwise the lawn was empty.

"You'll be going straight up to the residence, Sir?" one of the agents asked.

"Later, Bob. I want to go to the Oval for a while first. Can we light a fire in there?"

"Yes, Sir." The agent spoke into a microphone concealed in his right sleeve.

*

As the President stepped into the Oval Office, Adalberto Rodriquez, a White House steward, had just finished lighting a fire in the fireplace.

"Good evening, Sir," he said. "There's fresh coffee. Would you like something to eat?"

"No, thanks. Just coffee."

"Right away, Sir."

As the steward disappeared into the small kitchen next to the office, the President eased himself into the high-backed chair behind his massive desk. He stared at a gold-framed picture of his wife on the near right corner of the desk. She died the summer after he was re-elected to a second term. They kept her cancer a secret during the campaign, always hoping she would beat the odds and recover. He briefly considered resigning when she died but knew that was only an expression of self-pity.

The steward re-entered the office and sat a tray with a cup of coffee and a silver carafe containing more on the desk. No sugar, heavy cream.

"That'll be all, Adalberto. Thanks."

"Just ring if you need me, Sir."

The president sipped the coffee for a minute or two, and then pressed a button hidden beneath the edge of his desk. A Secret Service agent opened a curved door and stepped into the office.

"I don't want to be disturbed for an hour or so. I'll buzz when I'm ready to go upstairs."

"Yes, Sir," the agent said. He turned and walked back out of the office, quietly closing the same curved door behind him.

The President then pressed a second button beneath the edge of his desk. It was linked to the White House surveillance center and shut down the hidden video cameras and audio recorders that recorded activity in the Oval Office. He had fought with the Secret Service for two weeks after he was first elected for the ability to make the office "dark" when he wanted privacy.

Finishing the coffee, the President rose from his desk and walked toward the fireplace, passing between two facing sofas. He turned to the left of the fireplace, placing his right hand on the frame of a painting of Thomas Jefferson. His fingers searched for a third hidden button.

CHAPTER 10

Bill and Paul were less tense as they drove back to Paul's house from the Cattle Guard. Agreeing on a course of action had cleared the air between them, Bill thought. And Paul was beginning to act like a bit like his old self as they approached his lane, darkened by the shadows of overhanging trees despite the clear night and a full moon.

Bill pulled his car in front of the log house, all its windows as dark as the lane.

"Didn't we leave the living room light on?" Bill asked as he cut the car's engine and switched off its headlights.

"I thought so. But I guess one of us must've clicked it off and forgotten."

"I guess."

They walked toward the front door. It was standing half open.

"I know we locked the door," Paul said. His voice was developing a nervous edge.

"You're right. If there a flashlight in your Jeep?"

"Yeah. Hold on."

Paul walked over to the Jeep and rummaged around under the front seat until he came up with a flashlight in a black rubber casing. He clicked it on. Its beam stabbed through the darkness, throwing a circle of light on the house's partly open front door.

Bill walked into the circle of light, reached inside the door to the left and switched on the living room light. He pushed the door the rest of the way open.

"Jesus H. Christ," he whispered. Paul moved in for a closer look, clicking off the flashlight.

"What the hell?"

The inside of the house had been torn apart. The sofa was on its back. Books were pulled off shelves. Tables were over-turned. Pictures were pulled from the walls and smashed onto the floor.

Bill headed toward the kitchen, crunching over broken glass. Suddenly he stopped, wondering if whoever did this might still be in the house. He took two more steps and picked up the receiver on the wall phone to call the Sheriff's office. The line was dead.

CHAPTER 11

The President pushed the portrait of Jefferson upward on concealed tracks in the wall behind the picture, revealing the front of a square, recessed wall safe almost the size of the painting. A spring-loaded bolt clicked into place, firmly holding the picture above the safe, which had two locks, each requiring a separate combination. He deftly opened both locks and pulled the safe door open, causing a small light inside to flick on.

Three manila envelopes were standing on their edges, side by side, on a rack in the middle of the safe's interior. The President pulled them out and walked back to his desk.

As he had done a half dozen times in the past two weeks, he first opened the nine-inch by twelve-inch envelope labeled "No. 1." Inside were two eight-by-ten glossy photographs of the surface of Mars. Information on the back of the photos identified them as pictures taken by the Viking I orbiter on July 25, 1976, of a mostly flat plain called Cydonia Mensae in Mars' northern hemisphere. The black and white photos were computer enhanced for clarity and colorized to more closely resemble the red planet's surface. The first picture showed a three-hundred-square-mile area of Cydonia. In the lower left were several mountains that looked like pyramids. The second picture showed a flat plain, about 10 miles across. In the upper right corner of the picture was what appeared to be a mile-wide sculptured face, staring skyward like a reclining Sphinx.

The President slipped the two pictures back into their envelope and sighed. These were the well-known pictures of the "face" and "pyramids" on Mars that were released to the public by NASA during the Viking missions. They graced the cover of every tabloid in the world and triggered a decades-long controversy. Some people believed them to be artifacts of a long-dead Martian civilization or evidence that aliens from an advanced civilization had visited Mars and built them. NASA scientists had long ago dismissed the images as tricks played by light and shadows.

The second envelope also contained two pictures, much like the first ones but with much higher resolution. Data on the backs of the photos identified them as taken by the Mars Observer spacecraft in 1993.

It was always at this point when looking at the pictures that a knot began to form in the President's stomach. According to NASA, the Mars Observer exploded as it approached Mars during the summer of 1993, just days before it was to become operational and begin photographing the planet's surface. Some fringe scientists and UFO groups had charged that the craft was not lost, that it had carried out its mission in secret, and that NASA, a civilian agency, had been quietly taken over by the Defense Department, all in an effort to conceal the truth about the face and pyramids. If these pictures are real, the President thought, then at least some of those charges must be true. And that meant he had been kept in the dark. By whom? Why?

He opened the top right drawer of his desk and pulled out a magnifying glass he had brought down from the residence when he had first gotten the photos. In a move that was becoming a ritual, he focused the glass over the picture with the overview of the Cydonia plain.

There, midway between the face and the mountains, or pyramids, was a black, triangular-shaped object. It looked like a wedge of pie. Except that, according to the distance scale on the photo, each of the object's three sides was nearly a quarter mile long.

*

The President put the magnifying glass on his desk and stood up, pushing the third envelope aside. He looked toward the open safe by the fireplace and then began to pace around the room, his hands stuck in his back pockets.

He knew he wasn't supposed to have these pictures. They were dangerous. Cole Favate, his childhood friend from Ohio and now an Air Force colonel assigned to the Defense Intelligence Agency at the Pentagon, had given them to him two weeks ago.

It was after a state dinner at the White House for the Italian prime minister. Cole and his wife, Karen, were at the dinner. Afterward, Cole asked the President if they could have a few words in private. The President led the way into the Oval Office, where he switched off the hidden video cameras and recorders.

Without saying a word, Cole pulled the three envelopes from inside his dress tunic and handed them to the President.

Only then did Cole speak. "I'm giving you these envelopes because you're my friend," he said. "They're self-explanatory. I can't say anything more about them except that I'm not supposed to have them, and you're not supposed to see them. My career—hell, my life—would be in danger if anyone knew. After you look at the contents, destroy them."

"Cole ..." the President began.

"Please, Mr. President," Cole interrupted. "Don't ask me anything. Just trust me and do as I say. We must never discuss this again."

Then Cole abruptly left, leaving the President dumbfounded and alone in the Oval Office with the three numbered envelopes.

The President then immediately locked them into his safe and walked back to the State Dining Room to say his farewells to the departing guests.

After midnight he returned to the Oval Office and opened the envelopes and studied the contents. He had repeated that exercise every few days since the dinner. He had no intention of destroying them. He also had no idea what to do with them.

*

The President rubbed his eyes and checked his watch. It was almost ten-thirty.

He stepped back to his desk, sat down and opened the third envelope.

Inside were four more pictures. The first was a duplicate of the Viking I photo of the Cydonia plane, with the pyramids in the lower left and the face in the upper right. The second was a photo of the face taken by the Mars Global Surveyor orbiting craft in April 1998. This was the picture that was released to the public and which NASA had said was conclusive proof that the face was only a trick of light and shadows. In this photo the face had none of the distinctive, sharp features of the Viking I and Mars Observer photos. It looked like a flattened pile of rubble with vague suggestions of a mouth and eyes. Hundreds of newspapers had run this photo next to the Viking I image, along with stories explaining that there never was a face, that it was all the result of light, shadows, and overactive imaginations: NASA had been right all along.

The third photo, also from the Mars Surveyor mission, had many lines of technical data printed on the back. It had taken the President several hours to figure out enough of it to know that the picture was taken by a different camera on the Surveyor: a high-resolution spy satellite camera, the kind that can distinguish individual auto license plate numbers from earth orbit. The camera wasn't even supposed to be on the craft. Its data was scrambled and beamed via a top-secret frequency back to satellite dishes hidden in the desert of central Australia.

The President needed no magnifying glass. Filling the eight-by-ten image was the face, like in the Viking I and Mars Observer photos, only extremely clear and sharp. There was no question of light or shadows. Or of natural phenomena. The structure was clearly artificial, a mile-wide face carved from the stone of the Martian surface: a mix of human and simian features, staring skyward. In this photo, both nostrils and the pupils of the eyes were clearly visible, along with individual teeth in a partly open mouth.

The President had a numb feeling in his chest as he reached for the final photo. It had also been taken with the Surveyor's secret spy camera.

It was another overview of the Cydonia plane, but much clearer. Where the single black triangular object had been in the Observer photo, there were now eight such objects. They were arranged in a circle formation, looking like a pie whose slices were slightly separated.

CHAPTER 12

When Bill headed for the kitchen, Paul turned to his left and opened the door to a closet next to the front door in the living room. He pulled a 12-gauge shotgun from the back and was getting a box of shells from a closet shelf when Bill came out of the kitchen.

"Whoa! Why do you have that cannon?"

"Dad left it to me." Paul slipped two shells into the gun's double barrels and snapped them shut. "Whoever did this might still be in the house. Did you call Dave Taylor?"

"The line's dead. Probably cut. My cell phone's in the bedroom. I forgot it when we went to dinner."

"I left mine at school. I've been too rattled and embarrassed to get it. Sharon took hers with her. Reception sucks out here anyway."

Armed with the shotgun, Paul and Bill first went into the guest room to get Bill's cell phone, which he had left on the bedside table next to his laptop. But they found it on the floor, smashed into a pile of plastic shards and wires. Neither the laptop nor anything else in the room appeared to have been touched.

Bill was stunned. *Whoever did this was not looking to steal anything. What were they after?*

They then moved from room to room, upstairs and down, turning on lights as they went, checking closets and under beds. Bill checked a telephone in Paul and Sharon's bedroom; it was dead, too. The damage was confined to the downstairs, mainly the living room and kitchen.

Bill and Paul took the flashlight outside, but nothing

seemed amiss except that the phone line had been cut where it came into the back of the house near the kitchen window: a two-foot section had been removed. There were some vague depressions in the damp grass near the window that looked like footprints. The loose gravel covering the driveway and parking area in front of Paul's house made it impossible to distinguish footprints or tire tracks.

"Whoever did this is long gone," Bill said, scuffing the soles of his shoes on the gravel. "Guess we'd better find a phone or drive to Dave's office and report this."

"Let's drive in. I don't feel like sitting here waiting for a patrol car to show up."

"Okay. Let me get a sweater. You cold?"

"No. I'm fine. I'll wait out here."

"You want me to put that gun back in the closet?"

"Nah. I'll hang on to it. Let's take it with us in the car. You never know."

"Yeah, I guess."

Bill turned and went into the house.

In the guest room, he sat on the edge of the bed to unzip his duffel and get his sweater. There, on the top of his clothes was a white envelope with his name on it. Only his name wasn't written or typed. It was made up of letters, in different type styles, which had been clipped out of newspaper headlines.

Bill tore the envelope open. Inside was a single sheet of white paper with a similarly constructed message: GO BACK TO NEW YORK. REMEMBER JANE.

Bill's hands were shaking as he refolded the paper and carefully put it back into the torn envelope, which he folded into thirds and stuck into his right back pocket, behind his wallet.

*

It was nearly midnight by the time they pulled into the parking lot of the Sheriff's office.

Paul pressed a buzzer at the office door. A night deputy

looked up from his desk, recognized Paul, and walked across the room to let them in. Paul introduced Bill.

"Yeah, Dave said you were in town," the deputy said to Bill. He immediately turned to Paul. "What brings you in here at this hour?"

"Somebody broke into my house and vandalized it earlier tonight."

"Jeez, I'm sorry to hear that. You've had enough problems as it is. I'll send somebody out, but it's gonna take a bit. We only got one deputy on patrol at night and he's busy on a case right now. In fact, Dave got called out of bed to help him."

"Anything serious?" Paul asked.

"It's Daniel Scott. The reporter. He committed suicide."

CHAPTER 13

The attic was dusty and full of cobwebs. Old boxes and suitcases were piled and scattered about, blocking Bill as he searched for a way out. Through a small dirty window he could see the Ohio River in the distance, like a silver snake twisting between banks of trees whose color was so intense that they glowed as if consumed by green fire. The cloudless cobalt sky threatened to swallow the entire scene.

Bill turned and there, right behind him, was the attic staircase he had been looking for. Confused, he walked down the ten steps into a hallway and found himself on the second floor of a house that seemed both familiar and unfamiliar at the same time. There were three bedrooms and a bathroom, their doors all open. The bathroom contained a large galvanized washtub and some small buckets, but no sign of any plumbing. In the bedrooms, old-fashioned rail beds were neatly made and covered with handmade multicolored quilts. Ornate oak dressers and chests of drawers, their tops bare, devoid of any personal effects, stood against the walls. Curtains were pulled back, exposing clean windows that looked onto a yard. From one of the bedrooms he could see a barn. Between the house and the barn was a flock of chickens, pecking in the dirt and scrubby grass. Next to the barn was a horseless buckboard.

Leading down to the main floor of the house was another staircase that ended in a central hall and the front door. Bill descended the bare wooden stairs, his footfalls echoing through the empty house.

Downstairs, a parlor and living room contained more oak furniture and some overstuffed chairs and red and blue braided rugs. A round oak table surrounded by six high-backed chairs stood in the center of the kitchen. Each place at the table was set with blue and white china dishes and polished silverware. There were more empty buckets on a counter. The floor was made of wide, highly polished pine boards. A black wood-burning stove was cold to the touch. This must be a movie set, Bill thought.

He was drawn to a door next to the stove. It opened onto stone steps leading to a cellar whose damp walls glowed softly. He could barely see down to where the stairs met the cellar floor.

Bill descended the cellar steps, his palms suddenly clammy and his throat dry. He was gripped by a rising fear that he didn't understand.

Once in the cellar, his fear intensified. Boxes and crates like those in the attic were piled around the underground room. The air was chilly and damp. He wanted to turn and run upstairs and out into the sunlight. But his feet would only carry him forward, toward the center of the cellar floor and a barely visible wooden trap door with a rope handle. He lifted the door on its rusty hinges and discovered another set of stairs leading to a deeper subterranean chamber. It was pitch black and he could hear water dripping.

Now he was truly seized with terror. His body seemed to work independently of his mind as he put his right foot on the first step and started down ....

Bill blinked awake, sunlight streaming onto his face from an open window above the bed. He was lying on his back, covered with perspiration; the sheets were tangled about his legs.

He looked at his watch. Ten-thirty. He rolled over on his right side. He could hear scraping sounds coming from the kitchen.

"Paul?"

"In here. Just a minute."

Bill looked around the small bedroom. His duffel sat open on a chair. Through the half-open bedroom door he could see into the living room. The sofa was on its back.

Bill's mind returned to the previous night. Dinner. The break-in. His smashed cell phone. The note in his suitcase. Driving to the Sheriff's office. Learning that Daniel Scott had killed himself. Returning to Paul's cabin at three a.m. with a bored and sleepy deputy sheriff who took some pictures and filled out a report. Bill had been so wound up when the deputy left that he finally took an Ambien to fall asleep. Paul went to his bedroom upstairs.

Bill hadn't told anyone about the note, not even Paul. Why ransack most of the house's first floor just to leave him a note? "Remember Jane" was clearly a threat. What else could it be? Was the break-in a way of emphasizing it? Why destroy his cell phone? Why not his computer?

But none of this answered an even bigger question. Why would anyone care, and care enough to threaten him with the name of his dead wife, because he was helping Paul find his lost daughter?

Tears formed in Bill's eyes as he thought of Jane. He wiped them away and sat up, swinging his legs over the edge of the bed. He hadn't bothered with his sleep shorts last night. About twenty minutes after taking the sleeping pill, he fell into bed in his underwear.

The rich smell of strong coffee caused him to look up. Paul was standing in the doorway with a steaming mug, which he offered to Bill.

"I hope you like it black. Somehow the coffee and coffee maker survived, but the milk and sugar were all over the kitchen floor. What a fuckin' mess."

Bill sipped the coffee slowly. Paul seemed chipper and cheerful. Too much so, Bill thought, and then let the thought pass.

"How well did you know Daniel Scott?"

"Well, he did all the Courier stories about Cindy. So, he talked to me some, but I didn't know him otherwise. He was the first black reporter the Courier ever hired. He was always fair and considerate. Of course, I never told him anything about the UFO. I can't believe he's dead."

"Paul, let's start checking the houses around here, but not until later in the afternoon. I want to go into town and talk to Graham Neal, and Dave. Why don't you stay here and straighten things up as best you can. I'll try to be back by two or three. That okay with you?"

"Sure. I could use some time to pull myself together. Anyway, I drove over to the neighbor's while you were sleeping and called the phone company. They said they'd send someone out by noon."

"By the way, I fired up my computer yesterday but I couldn't get a WiFi signal."

"I don't have WiFi. The computer in my office upstairs is linked directly into the cable-TV Internet modem through an Ethernet cable. But you should be able to hook your computer up to it. Just have to take your laptop upstairs."

"Okay. Nothing urgent. Maybe later."

After Bill shaved and showered, he put on a clean pair of slacks, a polo shirt, and a pair of sneakers. He pulled his wallet and the note from the back pocket of the pants he was wearing last night. He refolded the note and slipped it into his wallet.

Dave Taylor was oddly officious as Bill pulled up a chair in front of his desk.

"Dave, how did Daniel Scott kill himself?"

"Well, he parked his car along the riverfront, near the bandstand, and shot himself in the heart with a thirty-eight special revolver. The gun was in his right hand and his fingerprints were the only ones on it. Some kids who were out riding their bikes later than they should have been were the ones who found him. Looks like it happened shortly after midnight.

"We're doing an autopsy, but only because the family requested it. His mother is convinced he had a brain tumor that caused him to kill himself. The truth is hard to face."

"That's it? Nothing suspicious?"

"Nope. Why, does Paul think he was killed by a UFO?"

"Come on, Dave."

"Okay, I'm sorry. That was a cheap shot. No pun intended. It's just that things are getting a little weird. UFO reports, a missing girl, a break-in at Paul's in which nothing was taken, and now a suicide. This is a little town, Bill. That's a lot for my department to deal with."

"Do you have any idea what Daniel Scott had been doing in the hours before he killed himself?"

"I don't have a clue. Planning his suicide, I guess. Why don't you ask Neal?"

"I'm headed there right now. Did you know that Scott had been investigating the disappearance of Cindy Watson?"

"Well, shit, yes. I read the paper. What are you suggesting? A link between the girl and Daniel Scott?"

"No ... I don't know."

Bill started to ask the Sheriff why he hadn't mentioned the rash of UFO sightings but decided not to.

"Bill?"

"Yes."

"Is there anything you're not telling me? Remember our agreement?"

Bill shifted in his seat. He could feel the bulge of his wallet in his right hip pocket.

"No. There's nothing. Except that I don't have a cell phone anymore. Whoever broke into Paul's house smashed it."

Neal slumped in his desk chair. He looked like he had aged ten years and lost twenty pounds overnight. He was unshaved and his eyes were bloodshot.

"I just got off the phone with Daniel's parents in Denver. They're arranging to have the body shipped back there. But there's going to be a delay until Doc Halpin does the autopsy they wanted. Goddamn, what a sad day. I hired that kid right out of I.U. last year. He had all the makings of a great reporter. Gutsy guy. As an undergraduate he had been a leader in the African-American political caucus. He impressed me with his sense of calling, of purpose. He had been thinking about going into politics. But when I hired him and we shook hands, he said he thought he could have more influence as a journalist. His parents had been relieved. They thought journalism was a safer and happier career, away from bigotry and extremists. They believed it would give him a chance to do more good than running for a local office."

Bill had never seen the old man so distraught.

"Neal, if there's anything I can do ...."

"Thanks. But I think everything's under control. I wrote the story myself. It'll lead this afternoon's paper. Do you mind taking a rain check for dinner tomorrow? Maybe next week. You'll be here for a couple of weeks, right?"

"At least that long. No problem. Whenever you feel like it."

"How's Paul doing? I noticed on the police report that his house was broken into last night."

"Yeah. Strange. It was tossed, but nothing was taken. The phone line was cut."

"You're right. It is odd. But we're just going to include it in the routine police briefs. Paul's had enough publicity. I guess big city ways are finally catching up to Jefferson."

"I guess. Take care, Neal. If you need anything, you know where to reach me. Paul's phone should be fixed by now. Don't use the cell number I gave Sarah. Whoever broke into Paul's smashed my phone. I've got to get a new one."

"Okay. Thanks for dropping by."

"Neal, one more question. What was Daniel working on yesterday?"

"A farming story about the dry weather, as far as I know. I gave him a lot of room."

"Was he still looking into Cindy Watson's disappearance?"

"I don't think so. There wasn't much more to do on that story. We were just waiting for another development."

"Where did Daniel live?"

"At the Wayne Hotel. He had a room there. Number six, I think. He had some long-term deal that he said was as cheap as an apartment. It seemed to suit him."

"This Dr. Halpin is the county coroner?"

"Part-time. He's a G.P. Came here about five years ago from Phoenix. He used to moonlight in the coroner's office there. He's a good doctor, but a bit of an odd duck. James is his first name. James Halpin."

"Can I use a phone?"

"Sure. Use the one on Sarah's desk. She's gone home for lunch."

"Thanks."

Bill called the Madison County Memorial Hospital and learned that Dr. James Halpin was making rounds.

*

At the hospital, Bill waited in the emergency room after having Dr. Halpin paged.

"Bill Sanders?"

Bill turned and was met by a tall man in a lab coat with a stethoscope hanging from his neck. He was heavy-set with a neatly trimmed black and gray goatee. He was wearing wire-rimmed glasses, a bolo tie and cowboy boots made from alligator hide. He appeared to be in his sixties.

"Dr. Halpin. Thanks for seeing me on such short notice."

"It's a pleasure. I'm one of your fans. Always had a secret desire to be a writer myself. Dave Taylor said you were in town, and I was hoping I would get a chance to meet you. When I moved here five years ago, I started hearing a lot about you. All good, I might add."

"Thanks. I hope we can get together later under better circumstances. I'm here about Daniel Scott."

"That's real bad. That poor young man. I didn't know him well, but I would never have pegged him as suicidal."

"I wonder if I could see his body and whatever personal effects he had with him when he died?"

"I'm not sure. I'm not doing the autopsy until later today. What's your interest in this?"

"I'm an old friend of Paul Watson's, and I'm here to help him find his missing daughter. Daniel had been covering her disappearance, and I wondered if there was anything he knew that he hadn't put in his stories. I know it's a long shot, but I thought he might have some notes or something."

"Well, it's a little irregular but I guess it's okay. Come on."

Dr. Halpin led Bill through a corridor down some basement steps to the hospital's small morgue. The room contained an autopsy table and six stainless steel doors in a row. They looked like the front of squat refrigerators in a restaurant kitchen, except they were at waist level.

"What do you want to see first, the body or the effects?"

"The body, I guess."

*

What a waste, Bill thought, as he looked down on the body of Daniel Scott. He was handsome, in a scrawny kind of way, with strong features and close-cropped hair. The thirty-eight had left an ugly red entry wound, surrounded by powder burns, in the left center of his chest.

"No exit wound?"

"No. My guess is the slug was stopped when it hit a vertebra. I'll know for sure in the morning. Seen enough?"

"Yeah. What about his effects?"

Dr. Halpin rolled Daniel's body back into its refrigerated vault. He walked to the other side of the autopsy room and took a large plastic bag from a shelf and dumped its contents onto the bare autopsy table in the center of the room.

Aside from Daniel's clothes and shoes, there were car keys, two quarters, a wallet containing twenty-seven dollars, an Apple iPhone, a couple of credit cards, a driver's license, car registration, and an Indiana State Police press pass. A cheap Bic ball-point pen was bound to two new reporter's notebooks with a thick rubber band. Both notebooks were blank. The iPhone required a password. Bill examined the driver's license. Daniel Scott would have been twenty-four next month.

"Doctor, is there anything here that strikes you as out of the ordinary?"

"No, not really. The only thing I noticed is that he apparently knew more about human anatomy than the average suicide. A lot of people who shoot themselves in the heart don't really know precisely where it is. They often aim a little too far toward the center or a little too high or too low. They usually still manage to kill themselves, but not this neatly. It looks like Daniel knew exactly what he was doing or got lucky. A perfect kill shot."

As Bill left the hospital, he asked the emergency room receptionist for directions to the Wayne Hotel. It was only six blocks away.

Outside, dark clouds were threatening rain as Bill began walking in the direction of the hotel. He had gone only a couple of blocks when it suddenly began to sprinkle. But then just as suddenly the sun broke through and the clouds began moving off to the north.

Bill caught sight of the three-story Wayne Hotel from half a block away and remembered that when he was growing up in Jefferson it was a rooming house called the Olde Inn, mainly catering to transients. It was built as a large private home around the turn of the century but had fallen on hard times just after World War II. Now it had a fresh coat of white paint and red aluminum awnings over the windows. But as Bill got closer, he thought it still had the look of a rooming house trying to be a hotel.

Bill walked up three stone steps to the hotel's veranda. Through a screen door he could see a small, dim lobby. It seemed deserted. He pulled the screen door open and stepped inside.

There was no one in the lobby or behind the front desk. He could hear muffled conversation coming from a room somewhere in the back.

He looked behind the desk at a row of cubbyholes, each with a room number above it. Most were empty. The one for number six contained two pink message slips and a key. The key was attached to a wooden circle with the number 6 on one side and the hotel's name and address on the other. *Nothing electronic here.* Bill stepped behind the desk and pulled out the message slips. Both were for phone calls for Daniel Scott.

He pulled out the number six key and headed for the staircase. A sign indicated that rooms six through ten were on the second floor. He started up the stairs, his sneakers making little noise on the threadbare carpet.

Upstairs, he opened Daniel's room, slipped in and quietly closed the door behind him.

The room's two windows were closed; the air was stifling. Light filtered in through dirty panes that looked out onto an alley. The bed was unmade. On a desk was a laptop computer, still on, its screen saver displaying flashes of colored light. Bill tapped the space bar. Password protected.

Next to the computer was a stack of five manila file folders. The top file, labeled "Cindy Watson," contained clips of Daniel's stories about her disappearance.

The second file was labeled "UFO: Madison County."

Inside the second file was a folded topographical map of the county.

Bill unfolded the map. It was covered with a random pattern of Xs and Os. At the bottom of the map, apparently in Daniel's handwriting, were two notations: "O = UFO sightings" and "X = helicopters."

Most of the Os were right beside an X.

Bill looked at the area where Paul's house was located. Nothing.

He put the map back into the file folder and tucked it inside his shirt. The other files were labeled "City Council," "School Board," and "Chamber of Commerce." Bill ignored them. He took a hand towel from the bathroom and carefully wiped down everything he had touched.

He stepped out into the hallway as the door locked behind him. He paused at the bottom of the stairs. The lobby was still empty. He started toward the desk to return the key when a matronly-looking woman stepped into the lobby from the back room, where he had heard voices earlier.

"Oh," she said. "You frightened me. I didn't hear you come in."

"Sorry," Bill replied as he closed his hand around the key. "I was looking for a pay phone."

"Right behind you. It's usually for guests, though. But go ahead."

"Thank you."

The woman retreated back to a darkened room behind the front desk.

Bill turned to the phone and put his right hand into his pocket to get some change. He let the key fall in with his money and pulled out a quarter.

On a card by the phone were some numbers, including the Sheriff's office. Bill inserted his quarter, picked up the receiver and punched in the number.

A female voice answered, "Madison County Sheriff's Department."

"Dave Taylor, please."

"He's out. Can I help you?"

"This is a personal call. Do you know when he'll be back?"

"In about fifteen minutes. Can I take a message?"

"No thanks. I'll drop by."

The woman came out of the back room just as Bill replaced the receiver. He thanked her again and walked out onto the veranda and down the steps. His heart was pounding. The woman walked to the screen door and gave him a puzzled look as he headed down the street.

Two blocks from the hotel, Bill dropped the key into a mailbox. A block later he slipped the file folder marked "UFO: Madison County" from inside his shirt, removed the map, and threw the folder into a trashcan.

*

Dave Taylor was pulling his cruiser into a parking space reserved for the Sheriff as Bill walked into the parking lot.

"Back again? Did you talk to Neal?"

"Yeah, but he didn't know anything. Said Daniel had been working on a farming story yesterday."

"We'll probably never know the reason."

"Maybe. Dave, I have a favor to ask."

"What?"

"Can you order a paraffin test on Daniel Scott's right hand? It would show conclusively that he fired the gun, right?"

"Well, yes. But we already know that from his prints and the fact that he had the gun in his hand. I can't order a test like that—the State Police lab people would have to do it—unless there is suspicion of foul play, which there is not. Not to mention that I do have a limited budget. Why the hell would you want such a thing?"

"I can't really explain. I guess it's just a feeling, a hunch. You ordered an autopsy. Isn't that something you would only do if you suspected foul play?"

"Normally, yes. But his parents requested it and it was hard to say no to them. Anyway, it's something we can do locally without involving the State Police. And Doc Halpin doesn't charge that much."

"What if I offered to pay for the paraffin test?"

"That would raise too many bureaucratic problems."

"Dave, please do this. As a personal favor to me."

"You're getting to be a little high maintenance here ... oh, what the hell. It's a waste of time and money, but it won't be the first time the taxpayers' money was wasted. I'll call Indianapolis and see if they can do it tomorrow at the same time as the autopsy. But you owe me. Remember that."

CHAPTER 14

Bill returned to Paul's house around three-thirty. Paul's Jeep was in its usual spot, and the front door was unlocked, but there was no sign of Paul. The living room and kitchen had been more or less straightened up; missing pictures and a broken table leg were mute reminders of the earlier chaos. Bill lifted the receiver off the telephone in the kitchen and was relieved to hear a familiar dial tone. He hung up the receiver and walked back into the living room.

"Paul!" Bill shouted. No reply.

Bill went back out the front door and walked around the cabin to the back yard. Nothing.

He started to walk around the other side of the house when he heard a distant shout. Paul, emerging from a line of trees at the rear of the property, shouted again and waved. Bill met him in the middle of the back yard.

"I was wondering where you were."

"I took a walk just to get out of the house for a while and get some air."

Paul was winded and his face was flushed. His blue eyes seemed brighter than usual. When he got close, Bill could smell liquor on his breath.

"Are you okay?"

"Yeah, I just needed some air."

"Is something wrong?"

"Well, I don't know. Maybe. The telephone man came to fix the line and said he was confused that a two-foot section had been cut out. He had to string a whole new cable. He said whoever did this could have just cut the line to disable the phone. They didn't need to remove a section of it."

"What does that mean?"

"He said it was possible that whoever cut the line wanted to remove some kind of electronic device that had been attached earlier. Like a listening device."

"You mean he said your phone was bugged?"

"Well, I guess, in so many words. But he said it's impossible to know for sure."

"Jesus Christ. Who the hell would want to tap your phone?"

"I don't know." Paul's eyes darted around like a cornered animal's.

The rest of the afternoon and most of Wednesday, Bill and Paul drove around in Paul's Jeep and visited every house they could find within a mile or two. Because woods surrounded Paul's cabin, none of the people who lived in the area could see it from their houses.

Had anyone seen anything out of the ordinary around the time of Cindy's disappearance? Any unusual phenomenon? Any lights or sounds? Anything in the sky?

Most of the people with whom they spoke had already been questioned in the days after Cindy disappeared. But they seemed not to mind being questioned again. Most said they understood that Paul would want to do everything in his power to find his daughter. They seemed a little surprised by some of the questions, especially when asked if they had seen anything in the sky in the middle of the night.

By early Wednesday afternoon, Bill and Paul were getting nowhere. All their questions were answered with a shake of the head. Most people had been in bed asleep when Cindy disappeared. Those who weren't sleeping were inside watching television or reading, not out looking at the sky.

It occurred to Bill that what people said they were doing was perfectly normal. Most people aren't out at night looking at the sky, especially late at night. He remembered the last time he had really studied the night sky. It was years ago in South America when he was researching *Points South*. He and Jane had been in a rural mountain town in Argentina. They had just stepped out of a restaurant after a late dinner when a power failure plunged the little town into total darkness. There was no moon that night, and without the distraction of artificial light, the night sky suddenly became an overpowering, mesmerizing presence. The stars were bright and thick, the Southern Cross a four-cornered beacon. He and Jane had rushed back to their hotel and climbed six flights of stairs in the dark to get to the roof for a better view. From there they could see the full sky and stars all the way to the horizon. When the power came back on an hour later, they both had stiff necks from staring skyward. Later they agreed that the sight of the sky that night was as close as either had ever come to a religious experience.

But this search, Bill thought to himself, was turning into a futile experience. Finally, around two o'clock, Bill and Paul decided to visit two more houses and call it a day.

The first house was part of a small farm at the base of a steep hill that was the highest point in Madison County. No one was home.

They started up a steep gravel road to the second house, perched atop the hill.

"Ralph Johnson used to live there until he died last year," Paul said as he maneuvered his Jeep around a pothole. "I don't know who bought the place. It's no good for farming, but it has a great view."

"I see what you mean," Bill said as they pulled into the driveway of the house. From the front yard they could see south all the way to the Ohio River and beyond it to Kentucky. Bill looked in the direction of Paul's house, but could see nothing but thick woods.

Paul parked behind an old Chevrolet pickup. They started toward the door when it opened and a man in a blue uniform stepped out to greet them.

Bill thought the man was a policeman until he noticed the details of the uniform and realized he was a security guard.

"Howdy," the man said with a broad smile. "I heard you pull up. What can I do for you?"

Paul introduced himself and Bill and explained what they were doing. The man's name was Sam Wiggins and he was a security guard at a small electrical-parts factory in Jefferson.

"I read all about your daughter, Mr. Watson," he said. "Sure is a sad thing. I hope you find her okay. But I ain't gonna be much help. I work nights, four to twelve. I always stop for something to eat at Hink's, so I don't get home until a little after one. I'm leaving for work a little early today because I have to stop at the hardware store to get some washers for my kitchen faucet. Damn thing won't shut off."

"Mr. Wiggins, you've lived here for about a year, right?" Bill asked.

"Yeah. Moved here right after my wife died. We lived in town, but I couldn't stand to stay in that house alone. Our son lives in Louisville."

There was an awkward silence before Bill continued.

"Did the police question you about the missing girl?"

"Nope. But I heard they was talking to a lot of folks around here. Guess they didn't want to drive up here. Or maybe they came when I was working."

"Have you ever seen anything strange around here when you come home at night?"

"Like what?"

"Anything. Noises. Lights. Anything unusual in the sky?"

"You ain't one of them UFO people, are you?"

"No. I lived here when I was a kid. Paul and I went to school together and I'm just trying to help him find out what happened to his daughter. What UFO people are you talking about?"

"Well, some damn fool kids reported that they saw UFOs and some out-of-town folks—said they was researchers—was prowling around here this winter asking people about it. They never tried to talk to me. It's a good thing. I would've run them off the property. I don't want to wind up in no newspaper story and be laughed at."

"Don't worry. This is just a conversation among the three of us. And that's where it'll stay. But have you seen anything? It could be important, Mr. Wiggins."

"You sure this is just between us?"

"I swear it."

"Absolutely," Paul added.

"Well, four or five times when I've come home from work at night I've seen these funny shafts of light. First time it happened I thought it was one of them big searchlights you sometimes see car dealers using when they have a big sale or something. Only the beam was too wide.

"Usually these shafts of light seemed to go from the ground to a low cloud overhead. But sometimes I couldn't tell if the light went from the ground to the cloud or the other way around. Mostly they were way off in the distance, but once one was real close—a half mile away, maybe. It was spooky. The light didn't look like regular light. It was too intense. Almost looked solid. Then after a few seconds or minutes they would just blink out. Disappear.

"I never told nobody about this before. The next morning after I had seen one of these lights, I was always a little confused. Like maybe I was remembering a dream. I ain't nuts, Mr. Sanders."

"No, Mr. Wiggins, you're not. When was the last time you saw these lights?"

"Back in March, I reckon."

"Can you think of anything else you've seen? Or is there anything else you remember about the lights?"

"No, just the helicopters."

"What helicopters?"

"Right after I saw two of them lights, I heard helicopters in the distance. I never could see them. But they were there. It's hard to mistake that thump-thump-thump sound for anything else."

*

It was shortly after four when Bill and Paul arrived back at the cabin. They had said little to each other after their conversation with Sam Wiggins. Paul was clearly upset, and Bill didn't know what to say—or think. Except that something very strange was going on in Jefferson, and Dave Taylor might be in over his head.

There was a message on Paul's answering machine: "Paul, it's Dave Taylor. Could you have Bill Sanders give me a call?"

Bill punched in the Sheriff's office number from the kitchen phone.

"Madison County Sheriff's Office," the receptionist answered.

"Dave Taylor."

"Who's calling please?"

"Bill Sanders."

"Oh, Mr. Sanders. He's been trying to reach you. Hold on."

Paul came into the kitchen with a bottle of Scotch and began pouring himself a drink. He motioned for Bill to join him. Bill shook his head. Bill glanced at Tuesday afternoon's Courier on the kitchen table. There was a big photo of Daniel Scott at the top of the page. The headline, "Courier Staffer Dead," made no mention of suicide. Presumably the details were in the story.

"Bill?"

"Hi, Dave. What's up?"

"Dr. Halpin finished the autopsy on Daniel Scott, and the State Police did the paraffin test."

"And?"

"The autopsy results were what we expected. Daniel died from a bullet wound to his heart."

"The paraffin test?"

"Well, I give you high marks for hunches. It was negative. Daniel Scott did not fire that gun. We went back and checked out his Honda again. The gun was not fired inside the car either.

"We're now treating this as a homicide. Looks like he was shot and then placed in the car with the gun in his hand. We're running ballistics tests, but I'm sure the gun in his hand was the one that was used to kill him."

"Holy shit! Are there any suspects or motives?"

"Not yet. But the State Police are now officially on the case with us. I've got to call Daniel's parents and tell them the news and that we have to keep the body for I don't know how long. I guess in one sense they'll be relieved that he didn't kill himself."

CHAPTER 15

Paul was pouring himself a second drink as Bill hung up the phone.

"Daniel Scott didn't commit suicide. He was murdered and his body put in his car with the gun in his hand. Dave says the State Police are now in on the case."

Paul's hand holding his drink began to shake. He walked into the living room and sat down on the sofa.

"What the hell is going on, Bill? My daughter disappears. I see a UFO and hear a helicopter. My phone was probably tapped. A neighbor sees strange lights and hears helicopters. A reporter's killed."

Bill considered telling Paul about the note he had found in his suitcase and the map he took from Daniel's room, but decided to wait.

"Listen. I want to go talk to Dave. I would suggest you come, but you're working on your second Scotch and I don't think it would be wise to show up at the Sheriff's office with booze on your breath."

"You're right. Go ahead. I'll stay here. Let's go out to dinner when you get back. Cattle Guard again? It's the best around."

"Sure. That'd be great. Give me a couple of hours."

Dave Taylor, despite his measured speech, was clearly rattled. He shifted uncomfortably in his desk chair as Bill came into his office.

"This is a goddamn shame. Who would want to murder Daniel Scott? What the hell made you suspect it?"

"I told you. Just a feeling. A reporter's sixth sense, I guess. Maybe it was because everybody kept telling me he wasn't the suicidal type."

"Well, whatever it was, I thank you. I guess."

"Does Neal know?"

"Yeah, I just got off the phone with him. It's too late to get the story in today's paper. But it'll be on TV this evening. Those TV bastards have been calling from Louisville, Indianapolis, and Cincinnati. It's on the wires, too."

"Are you still going to have Paul Watson take a lie detector test this week?"

"Not possible now. Sorry, but that situation has to go on the back burner for a couple of days."

"Dave, how many helicopters are there in Madison County?"

"Are you sure you're not holding something back on me?"

"No. It's just that in checking around the last couple of days I've come across people who say they've heard helicopters out in the country at odd hours. I just wondered."

"Well, the State Police have one that sometimes operates out of their barracks about twelve miles east of here. Hap Slocum has one at the airport that he used to use for crop dusting, but something happened to the engine last fall and I don't think he ever got it fixed."

"No military helicopters?"

"I guess the closest military stuff would be the National Guard in Louisville. They sometimes fly over here. Maybe that's what people heard."

"Probably. It makes sense."

Bill left the Sheriff's office with the intention of walking over to the Courier to see Neal. But it was after five and he suddenly realized he was tired and hungry and wanted nothing more than dinner and a bed. He unlocked his rental car and headed toward Paul's.

About two miles out of town he heard a police siren behind him. In the rear view mirror he saw Dave Taylor in his brown and tan cruiser, motioning him to pull over.

Dave was out of breath.

"Got a call just after you left. Paul's been in a wreck. Drove his Jeep off the road into a concrete culvert about a mile north of his house. The deputy said he smelled like a distillery. He's in bad shape. Come on. We'll meet the ambulance at the hospital."

Bill left his car beside the road and jumped into the cruiser.

Dr. Halpin was working on Paul in the emergency room when they arrived at the hospital. A nurse made them wait in an adjoining room.

Another nurse came out.

"Dr. Halpin says Mr. Watson's real critical. I'm sorry. He says you can come in."

Dr. Halpin met Bill and the Sheriff at the door to the treatment room.

"Brace yourself. This ain't pretty. He's got a broken leg and hip and his chest is crushed. Plus, there's head trauma. But he's conscious. Barely. He's asking for you, Mr. Sanders. Hurry, before it's too late."

The doctor turned and went back into the treatment room.

"Go ahead," the Sheriff said. "I'll wait here."

Paul was on a surgical table. His clothes had been cut off and were in a heap on the floor. He was partially covered with a bloody sheet. The right side of his head was a mass of blood and hair. A sliver of his skull was visible.

Bill closed his eyes for a second, afraid he was going to faint.

He leaned over Paul, who was trying to say something. Blood and saliva ran from his partially open mouth. He reeked of alcohol.

"Bill?" Paul whispered.

"I'm here, Paul. Try to be still."

Across the table, Dr. Halpin jammed an intravenous injection into Paul's right arm.

Paul tried to speak again. Bill leaned over and put his ear next to Paul's mouth and held his left hand.

"... 'copter," Paul said in a ragged, barely audible whisper.

Suddenly Paul shuddered and his eyes rolled back in his head.

"Move back!" Dr. Halpin shouted. He pulled the sheet from Paul's bloodied chest.

Bill left the room and went back to where Dave Taylor was standing. He looked at Dave and shook his head.

Dr. Halpin came out five minutes later.

"I'm sorry," he said. "I did everything I could. The injuries were too massive. Nothing could've saved him."

CHAPTER 16

"Nancy?"

"Bill! Where are you?"

"Still in Indiana."

"Are you still staying with your friend?"

"No, I'm at a hotel."

"Is anything wrong?"

"It's Paul Watson. My friend. He was killed in a car wreck last week."

"Oh, Bill. I'm sorry. Are you all right? Is there anything I can do?"

"I'm fine. He was alone in his car. He ran off the road and hit a culvert."

"Why did he want you to come out there?"

"His ten-year-old daughter disappeared. Almost a month ago, now. He wanted me to help him find her. We were working on it when he was killed."

"I suspected as much."

"What do you mean?"

"Well, after our lunch just before you left, I kept thinking I had heard of Jefferson, Indiana, somewhere. It just kept rattling around in my heard. At first, I assumed it was simply part of your bio that I was remembering. Finally, I Googled it and found I was remembering it from a short CNN story about a girl's disappearance—her name was Cindy Watson—a couple of weeks before our lunch. I wondered why you didn't know about it until I realized you had been in remote areas of Asia for a month."

"Well, your suspicions were correct. I only found out about Cindy when I got to Indiana, just before I saw Paul."

"When are you coming back to New York?"

"Not right away. Maybe in a couple of weeks or so. At the funeral yesterday I promised Paul's wife I would stick around for a while and help her tie up some loose ends. Maybe continue to look for the daughter. The Sheriff thinks she's a runaway. I'm not so sure."

"You mean you think she was abducted."

"Yeah, maybe ... I don't know. It's a confusing situation. I'll fill you in on all the details when I get back. By the way, my cell phone is broken. I've got to get another one."

"That explains why you didn't return my calls."

Nancy then brought him up to date on the latest plans for his publicity tour in the fall for *Look Down*. She also told him she was in formal negotiations with some Hollywood producers for the film rights to the novel. Before they hung up, he gave her the phone number of the Jefferson Hotel where he was staying. He assured her he would get a new cell phone soon.

He called Hertz and arranged to keep the rental car for at least another two weeks.

Bill had moved out of Paul's house the same evening Paul died. Sharon and her parents had come down from Indianapolis by nine that night. Bill said he was moving to a hotel so they would have more room. The truth was, as usual in times of stress or crisis, he needed solitude.

He wanted to think things through and try to decide what to do next. He had never shown the note he found in his suitcase to anyone, or the map he took from Daniel Scott's room. In the case of the map, he knew that he might be withholding potential evidence in a murder case. But he also knew that if he showed it to Dave Taylor that would open up the whole UFO thing, clearly not a subject that pleased Dave or about which the Sheriff had an open mind. The same was true for Neal. And the last thing Bill needed was for the local Sheriff and the newspaper editor to think he was a UFO nut. But all the trails he tried to follow in his mind kept coming back to that forbidden topic.

Then there was the business of the helicopters. What the hell was that all about? Were they just National Guard helicopters from Louisville? Why did Daniel have them plotted on the county map? How could they be associated with UFO sightings?

And Paul's last word to Bill was "'copter." Was he trying to say that he wanted to be evacuated in a medical helicopter to a more sophisticated hospital? Or was he remembering the helicopter he said he heard the night of Cindy's disappearance, or the conversation they had with Sam Wiggins, the security guard? Or did he mean something else?

Sharon seemed genuinely glad that Bill had come to Jefferson, and she was clearly grief-stricken over Paul's death. A missing child and a dead husband within the span of a month took its toll. Yet there was a cold center to her he had never known before. Of course, he hadn't really known her, or of her relationship with Paul over the last twenty years. He hadn't, for instance, known about Paul's drinking problem. He decided not to tell Sharon that he knew Paul's account of Cindy's disappearance or what he and Paul had been up to when Paul was killed. She would have to bring it up first.

Although he had readily agreed, Bill was a little surprised after the funeral on Monday when Sharon had asked him to stay in town for a while longer. Paul's affairs appeared to be pretty much in order, and his life insurance policy was big enough to pay off the house and leave Sharon enough to live on. She could work if she needed to; she had been an English teacher at Jefferson High School but hadn't taught since a few months before Cindy was born. Plus, her parents—her father was a lawyer, her mother a doctor—were well off.

Maybe she just needs someone to talk to. Well, so do I. Someone who could help me figure out what the hell is going on. But who?

✳

Bill looked again at copies of Paul's death certificate and accident report. The cause of death was listed as accidental.

There was no reference on the police report to his having been drinking at the time of the crash. *Small towns take care of their own*. The report simply said Paul had lost control of his Jeep on Madison County Road No. 641 and struck a large concrete culvert at approximately five o'clock last Wednesday afternoon. No one knew where he was going or what he was doing out there. A local insurance salesman who was on his way to a client's farm came on the accident scene within minutes of the crash. The investigating deputies estimated Paul's Jeep was traveling at sixty miles an hour when it struck the culvert.

Bill had talked to the salesman on Thursday, the day after the crash. The man had told him exactly what was written on the police report: He was driving to a client's farm, heading north on 641, when he discovered the accident only minutes after it happened. He called the Sheriff's office on his cell phone. He said he considered trying to help Paul but was afraid to move him after he saw how badly he was injured. After the patrol cars and an ambulance arrived, he gave a statement and continued on his way.

Bill had also visited the crash site on Thursday, but decided to take another, closer look. He also wanted to see Paul's Jeep.

After talking to Nancy Luke, he left the hotel and drove to an auto junkyard on the outskirts of town where the police report said the Jeep had been towed. The junkyard was a big field, mostly covered with bent and twisted auto bodies in various states of rust and decay. Paul's Jeep, or what was left of it, was near a dingy-looking trailer that apparently served as an office. No one seemed to be around.

Bill walked over to the Jeep. It was nearly bent double. The two front tires were ruptured, and the smashed windshield was in the front seat. There was dried blood everywhere. One of Paul's shoes was wedged between the front passenger seat and the gearshift console.

Bill took a roundabout route to the crash site to avoid driving by Paul's cabin. He didn't want to risk a chance encounter with Sharon or her parents. He wasn't in the mood for conversation.

He came on the site from the north, the opposite way Paul had been traveling. The culvert Paul struck was about four feet in diameter and ran under the road, allowing water to drain to and from two huge cornfields on either side of the road. Bill parked his car and walked to the east side of the culvert. The impact had broken off a three-foot section of concrete and there were red paint marks on it and the culvert from the Jeep.

About a hundred feet out in the east field, a farmer was bouncing along on a noisy tractor, plowing. Bill waved and started walking toward him.

The farmer returned his wave and stopped the tractor. The diesel engine rattled as he shut it off.

"Hey!" Bill shouted. "Got a minute?"

"Sure," the farmer replied. "I never pass up a chance to stop working for a few minutes." He took of a pair of thick glasses and wiped sweat off both lenses with a handkerchief.

Bill shook hands and introduced himself. The farmer's name was Joshua Baker.

"I'm a friend of Paul Watson. He's the guy who was killed out here last Wednesday."

"I know. Poor guy. He helped get my daughter into college two years ago. Real sad. I was out here plowing when it happened. This on top of his daughter missing. His wife must be going through hell."

"Did you see the crash?"

"No. I was at the far edge of the field, where the land tilts down a bit. Too low to really see the road. I didn't really know anything had happened until I saw the flashing lights from the police cars and ambulance. By the time I got over there, the ambulance had taken him away and a tow truck was hooking up to the Jeep."

"Did the police question you?"

"Nope. Like I said, I didn't really see nothing. There was a deputy there with the tow truck guys, but he never said nothing to me. Just motioned me to get back out of the way."

"Did you hear the crash?"

"No way. Not with my tractor going. And I was half deaf from that helicopter flying so low and making all that racket."

"Helicopter?"

"Yes sir. About ten or fifteen minutes before I saw the flashing lights there was this big helicopter flying real low along the edge of the road, like it was looking for something. I figured it was the power company checking lines. But it was a weird-looking thing. It was all black and didn't have no markings. And the windows was all dark. Like them limousines you see on TV.

"Like I don't have enough goddamn problems. Neal and the paper are bustin' my chops to find Daniel Scott's killer. But I don't have anything that even faintly looks like a clue, not to mention a suspect or a motive. Now you come in here and tell me that Paul was killed by some big mysterious helicopter that swooped down and forced him off the road."

Bill had known this wasn't going to be easy.

"Look, Dave, this farmer, Mr. Baker, just told me what he saw. Why would a helicopter be flying over the road just before the crash? Why were its windows blacked out? Why didn't it have markings?"

"Josh Baker couldn't tell a helicopter from a camel! He can't see shit, even with his glasses on. You want to know how reliable a witness he is? Last year he shot his neighbor's German shepherd dead in broad daylight because he thought it was a wolf. The poor dog was only a few feet in front of him. A wolf! Never mind that there haven't been any wolves around here for God knows how many years.

"You were right about Daniel. But don't push it. Who the hell would want to kill Paul and who has the money to do it with a big expensive helicopter? Maybe it was one of those National Guard choppers from Louisville. And Josh's first reaction could have been right: maybe it was the power company checking lines. Hell, Josh could have seen a buzzard. They're black!"

By now Dave Taylor was shouting. He paused, swallowed, and forced himself to calm down.

"You asked me about helicopters in the county earlier, before Paul was killed. Does that have anything to do with this?"

"No. I had just heard some people talk about helicopters. That's all. What about Paul's last words to me?"

The Sheriff sighed and looked at the ceiling for a few seconds.

"A man who is in shock and dying might say anything. And don't forget he'd been drinking. A lot. I put a lid on that. I hope I don't regret it. Maybe you misunderstood him. Maybe one of the ambulance crew said something about this guy needing a Medivac helicopter and Paul was trying to repeat it."

Bill wanted to tell him about the helicopters Sam Wiggins had heard and about the helicopter Paul said he heard at the time of his UFO sighting. But it would only have enraged Dave Taylor and made Bill look like a head case.

"Okay. You may be right. But promise me something. Stop by Mr. Baker's and ask him about this in the next couple of days."

"Sure, sure," the Sheriff said, waving Bill out the door.

Bill stopped by the library to catch up on the news in The New York Times. Sunday's paper carried a profile of former United States Senator Warren Holden of New Mexico.

"Of course!" Bill said aloud.

The only other person in the reading room, an elderly lady searching through a stack of Time magazines, gave him a disapproving glance.

CHAPTER 17

It was almost six o'clock when Bill left the library and headed back to his hotel to call Warren Holden in Santa Fe. *I've got to get a new cell phone. Why do I keep putting it off?* The time difference meant Holden would probably still be in his office.

Warren Holden was a wealthy New Mexico lawyer and liberal Democrat activist who had served two terms in the United States Senate. A former Green Beret with close ties to the intelligence community, he had sat on the Senate Intelligence Committee during his second term; fluent in Spanish, his area of interest was South America. Fed up with Washington politics after twelve years in the Senate, he had decided not to run for a third term almost four years ago and had returned to his law practice in Santa Fe.

When Bill started working on *Points South* he contacted Holden, who was in his second term. The senator gave him many hours of background interviews about Latin and South America politics and United States intelligence operations in the region. The book's success was in no small way due to the insights provided by Holden, and Bill knew it. They became friends, although they had only spoken briefly by telephone twice since Holden had returned to New Mexico, most recently when Jane was killed.

Holden was a maverick who fought with members of his own party almost as much as he did with the Republicans. He was direct and honest. That, as much as anything, explained his ability to be a progressive liberal and at the same time remain close to a lot of button-down conservatives in the CIA, the National Security Agency, and various military intelligence operations. His decision not to run for re-election and his move back to Santa Fe did nothing to loosen those ties: he had barely started packing for the move west when he agreed to become an unpaid consultant to the director of the CIA.

Now Bill wanted—and needed—Holden's help again. But this time he wanted to talk to Holden about UFOs and helicopters. And recent events in Jefferson. The Times article, in a one-paragraph reference, had reminded Bill that Holden had an interest in UFOs and had once headed a Senate subcommittee that held hearings on the phenomenon. The subcommittee had concluded that more study was needed.

*

Back in his hotel room, Bill called Warren Holden's office in Santa Fe. A secretary said Holden was on another call and took Bill's number.

The phone rang five minutes later.

"Hello."

"Bill, it's Warren Holden. How the hell are you?"

"Good, Senator. Yourself? It's been awhile."

"Sure has. Time has a way of getting away. I'm doing 0kay. Busy as sin. Not as exciting as the Senate, but a damn sight less aggravating. You know, I was just wondering about you last week. I saw an item in Time magazine about your novel. When's it coming out? This fall?"

"Yes. Late September, I think."

"Looks like you got another winner on your hands."

"I sure hope so."

"So what can I do for you?"

"I need your help. Or at least your advice."

"You got it. Shoot."

For the next half hour Bill summarized all that had happened since he had received Paul's call for help. He held nothing back. He told Holden of the threat he had received, Paul's story, the UFO sightings, the helicopters, Daniel Scott's murder, and his suspicion that Paul may have also been killed.

When he finished, there was a long pause before Holden spoke.

"Jesus, boy, you've landed in the middle of a mess. You've stepped through the looking glass with the UFO thing. Be careful. You know what happens to people's reputations when they get involved with this stuff? You can get branded a nut case real quick like."

"I've noticed. What should I do?"

"Well, let me do some checking from this end. Call me back in a week or so. In the meantime, why don't you talk to Walter Jansen?"

"Walter Jansen? The guy who was an aide to Jimmy Carter?"

"None other. He always kept a low profile but was a lot closer to Carter than the press or public knew. You know him, don't you?"

"Well, I've met him a few times and interviewed him once, but I don't really know him. He was younger than Carter, but he still must be in his mid-or late-eighties."

"He should at least talk to you. If you need me to run interference with him I will. He owes me a couple of favors. He lives in Atlanta, and he's on the board of the Carter Center. Go talk to him in person. Don't try to do this on the phone."

"Why Jansen?"

"Not many people know it, but he's into UFOs. He's convinced they're real. Remember when Carter claimed to have seen one when he was governor of Georgia? Walter was with him at the time. That started his flying saucer interest. He convinced Carter to promise to dig into the UFO business if he was elected president and release everything to the public. Of course, not long after moving into the White House, Carter clammed up and never talked about UFOs in public again. But I'll bet he talked to Walter. And I'll also bet there's a cache of UFO files at the Center that aren't available to the public. They could be very interesting. After all, who the hell has more access to information than a president?"

"I guess. I vaguely remember reading about Carter's UFO sighting. Okay. I'll try to call him and arrange to fly down there later in the week."

"One other thing. Stay away from the usual UFO crowd, especially the UFO organizations and 'ufologists.' They're a bunch of asshole publicity hounds who don't do much but fight with each other over who's for real and who is and isn't a government informer. They think every light and plane in the sky is a UFO and the government is covering it up. Don't get stuck in their tar pit."

"So, we'll talk again?"

"Yep. Call me here next week."

Bill said good-by and hung up the phone. Only then did he wonder if his hotel phone could be tapped.

He lay back on the bed, unable to shake an eerie feeling that Holden was holding something back. But he couldn't put his finger on it. A cache of UFO files? Should he take the warning about ufologists at face value? Should he heed it? Surely everyone studying UFOs wasn't delusional. What about the UFO people who had come to Jefferson? He had been thinking of contacting them.

And Walter Jansen! That was a quantum leap in advice. But Holden was right. Jansen had been as close to Carter as anyone. And his interest in UFOs probably made him at least worth taking to. If he would talk.

Bill thought back on Carter's UFO sighting. It had been, as best he could remember, in the late 1960s or early 1970s.

The hotel's WiFi was slow and unreliable. Bill was at the library when it opened Wednesday morning. He spent the next two hours hunched over a microfilm reader looking at back issues of the Times and some news magazines; he also used a library computer to search the Internet.

The Carter sighting had been in October 1969 in Leary, Georgia. For some reason, it wasn't until 1973 that Carter filed a report on the sighting with the National Investigations Committee on Aerial Phenomena, or NICAP. A dozen friends, including Walter Jansen, who were with him at the time also saw the UFO, which Carter described in his report as "bright as the moon" at one point. Skeptics subsequently dismissed the sighting as Venus.

During his presidential campaign in 1976, Carter had said of his UFO sighting: "It was the darndest thing I've ever seen. It was big, it was very bright, it changed colors, and it was about the size of the moon. We watched it for ten minutes, but none of us could figure out what it was. One thing's for sure. I'll never make fun of people who say they've seen unidentified objects in the sky."

He then made a promise: "If I become President, I'll make every piece of information this country has about UFO sightings available to the public and the scientists."

In 1977, shortly after he was sworn in, he asked the National Aeronautics and Space Administration to establish a panel of inquiry to investigate UFOs. NASA refused.

Carter never made any further comments about UFOs or his campaign promise. He refused to ever again discuss the subject, at least publicly.

It took three phone calls to the Carter Center in Atlanta to finally get through to Walter Jansen's assistant, an elderly-sounding woman named Ruth Simpson. She had been with the Carter Center from its beginning and knew Bill by reputation.

"President Carter always spoke highly of your South America book," she said.

"Thanks. I really need to see Mr. Jansen as soon as possible."

"He's not in today, but he'll be here tomorrow. If you hold, I can call his cell and see if he's available tomorrow. Can I tell him what this is about?"

"It's a personal matter."

"Very well. Hold please."

She was back on the line in a couple of minutes.

"He could see you tomorrow for half an hour at about three-thirty. Is that good for you?"

"I think so. I'm in Indiana. I'll try to get a fight to Atlanta either tonight or in the morning, but it shouldn't be a problem. I'll call back if it is."

"Very good. If I don't hear from you otherwise, we'll expect you at three-thirty on Thursday." She gave him the direct number for Jansen's office.

Bill booked a seat on Delta Air Lines flight 421 at eleven o'clock the next morning from Louisville to Atlanta. He should be in downtown Atlanta by one or one-thirty. He booked a return flight for eight that night.

*

Bill decided to fly from Louisville because its airport was the closest one to Jefferson. Also, the flight times had been better for him than from Cincinnati or Indianapolis.

The forty-five-mile drive through the Southern Indiana countryside to Louisville should have taken less than an hour. Bill left Jefferson at eight-thirty to give himself plenty of time. By nine-twenty he was pulling onto Interstate 65 to cross the Ohio River to Louisville and the last few miles to the airport on the south edge of the city.

As he passed the last exit before the bridge, he realized something was wrong. He could see a pillar of oily black smoke ahead, rising through the bridge's girders and climbing against the blue sky; he had to brake hard to avoid crashing into the cars in his lane that were also screeching to a halt.

It took police and firemen more than two hours to clean up the debris and tow away three pickups that had caught fire in the middle of the bridge, blocking all southbound traffic. A car behind the trucks had skidded and hit the bridge railing.

A Kentucky state trooper walking back down the line of backed-up cars told Bill and other nearby drivers there were no injuries, just a "big mess to clean up."

"What about the drivers of the pickups?" Bill asked.

"Can't find them. The guy whose car hit the bridge said all three drivers stopped the trucks in the middle of the road and then jumped into a car that had stopped just in front of them. It took off like a bat out of hell just as the trucks burst into flames. Funny. Those were brand new trucks with dealer plates. Looks like somebody wanted to block traffic in a big way. We're looking for them."

It was nearly eleven-thirty by the time Bill was able to continue. He took the first exit after the bridge; a clerk in a donut shop let him use the store phone. *I'm going to get a new cell today. This afternoon.* A Delta agent confirmed the obvious: he had missed his flight. There was another flight at one, but it was full. He booked the eleven o'clock flight for the next day and called the Atlanta number Ruth Simpson gave him.

Jansen himself answered.

Bill explained what had happened and that he couldn't get to Atlanta until early the next afternoon.

"Can you meet me then?"

"What's this about?"

"I'd rather not say over the phone."

"I understand ... say, didn't you interview me several years ago when you were with The New York Times?"

"Yes, in D.C. Long after your White House years. But it was for background only. I wanted your insights into some Latin America politics Carter had been involved in for a book I was thinking of writing."

"The South America book?"

"Yes."

"Well, that was a good book. Still is. Jimmy loved it."

"Thanks."

"Look, I'll expect you tomorrow afternoon here at the center. Around three-thirty."

Before he hung up, Jansen gave Bill his cell phone number. Bill gave Jansen his, explaining the phone was broken but would be replaced soon. He also gave Jansen the number of the Jefferson Hotel.

CHAPTER 18

During the drive back to Jefferson, Bill started thinking how odd the incident on the bridge was. *Why would three men set fire to new trucks and then flee the scene in an obviously prearranged ride? Why did they want to block the bridge? To delay someone? Me? That doesn't make sense. No one knew where I was going. They would have had to know my exact location to trap me on the bridge. This is crazy, or at least paranoid.*

Bill switched on the car radio and scanned to WHAS, a big Louisville news station.

"... special report. Police tell WHAS they are searching for three men who blocked traffic for more than two hours by setting fire to three stolen pickups in the southbound lanes of the I-65 bridge over the Ohio River. The men fled the scene in a car driven ahead of the trucks by an accomplice. That car, a stolen white Chevrolet Malibu, was later found abandoned near Churchill Downs. The trucks, Ford 150s, were stolen early this morning from two separate dealers. A car that was traveling behind the trucks skidded and struck the bridge railing, but the driver was not injured. He was identified as Clay Irwin, thirty-three, of Clarksville, Indiana. He was one of several witnesses who saw the suspects flee the scene in the Chevrolet. We'll be following this story as it develops, so stay tuned. Now, for a look at today's weather ..."

Bill scanned for other stations but found nothing more about the story. He switched back to WHAS. He was only half listening to the radio as his mind raced through the morning's events. *Was the delay aimed at me? Will I be delayed again tomorrow? Who would, or could, do this?*

"... light rain early tonight over the Kentuckiana metro area ..."

"... town hall meeting scheduled for tomorrow afternoon ..."

*

Bill was almost halfway back to Jefferson before he calmed down and concluded that he was making too much of a simple coincidence. He reached down to turn off the radio.

"... other news. This just in. Former New Mexico Senator Warren Holden has died. His body was found in his car in a Santa Fe parking garage near his office this morning. Officials there say he apparently suffered a fatal heart attack."

CHAPTER 19

Dawn was beginning to break over the Manhattan skyline as Bill Sanders crossed the George Washington Bridge. He had been driving all night.

Traffic was light as he headed toward Eastside Towers, his apartment building on East Seventy-Second Street. He slowed as he drove past the building, looking for anything—he wasn't quite sure what—out of the ordinary. But all looked early-Friday-morning Manhattan normal. He headed downtown and parked his car in a garage on Forty-Second Street near the Lincoln Tunnel. He hefted his duffel bag and backpack out of the trunk and began walking east to the Algonquin Hotel on Forty-Fourth Street. Bill had called the afternoon before from the outskirts of Chicago and reserved a room for three nights, arranging for an early check-in.

Once in the room, he stripped, took a shower, shaved, and put on fresh clothes. He called room service and ordered coffee, orange juice, toast, and scrambled eggs. Waiting for the food, he realized he was probably being silly by not going straight to his apartment. He knew he had no experience or skills in cloak-and-dagger stuff. But if he was being watched or tracked, this might throw them off for a time. Whoever they were. He also realized he had no idea what he was doing or what was going on. If anything was going on. Could all that happened in the last few weeks be just a series of unrelated events?

His thoughts were interrupted by a knock, signaling his breakfast had arrived.

As soon as he had eaten, he picked up the phone and

punched in the number of the concierge desk at Eastside Towers.

"Eastside Towers. This is George. May I help you?"

"George, it's Bill Sanders."

"Mr. Sanders. How are you? Are you back in town?"

"Yes, but I won't be coming to my apartment for a while. I'm staying at the Algonquin Hotel for a few days. George, has anyone been asking for me? Have there been any messages."

"No, Sir. But we do have a FedEx overnight envelope that came for you ... yesterday? Yes, Thursday morning. I signed for it."

"Where's it from?"

"New Mexico. Santa Fe."

Bill felt a vise tighten around his chest. There didn't seem to be enough oxygen in the room. He sat down on the edge of the bed.

"Mr. Sanders?"

"I'm here, George. Sorry. Does the return label have a name or street address on it?"

"Just a street address. No name." When George read the address, Bill recognized it instantly.

"Listen, could you do me a favor?"

"Sure, just name it."

"Can you have that FedEx envelope sent to me at the Algonquin? Put it in one of those big manila envelopes with my name on it and have it delivered to the front desk of the hotel. I'll tell the desk clerk to be on the lookout for it and to call me as soon as it arrives."

"No problem. In fact, I'll deliver it myself when I take my lunch break at around noon. Is that okay?"

"Great, George. Take a taxi. I'll take care of you when I get back, if that's all right?"

"Of course, Mr. Sanders."

"And George ...."

"Yes, Sir?"

"Can we keep this between us? Don't tell anybody about the envelope or where you're taking it. Also, I don't want anyone to know I'm in town or at the Algonquin."

"Absolutely. No problem."

"Thanks, George. I won't forget this."

Bill hung up the phone and lay back on the bed and tried to calm himself and organize his thoughts.

The FedEx envelope was from Warren Holden. It was delivered overnight. That meant Holden sent it sometime on Wednesday, the day after I talked to him and the day before he was found dead. Had Holden discovered something? Why hadn't he simply called? But ... of course! He couldn't have. I was supposed to call him back next week and had not left a number or address in Jefferson. Holden had my cell number, but that was useless. That explains why Holden sent the FedEx envelope to New York. No use wondering what's in it. I'll know soon enough.

He tried to relax, but the events of the last twenty-four hours kept replaying in his mind.

Bill had headed back to Jefferson after missing his flight to Atlanta because of the pickup truck fires on the bridge. When he heard on the radio that Warren Holden was dead, he thought he was going to be physically ill. But he forced himself to keep driving.

Back in Jefferson, Bill had called Walter Jansen's cell number and was switched to voice mail. He left a message canceling their second appointment the next day, claiming a personal emergency. He promised to call back later and reschedule it. He quickly packed, checked out of the hotel and left town without a word to anyone. Talk to people and they die, he thought. If someone or something wanted him out of Jefferson, he was going to oblige.

He drove straight through to New York, but first went north to Chicago and took Interstate 80 east. Somebody always seemed to know where he was going; maybe this would confuse them. Would his simply leaving Jefferson satisfy whoever had put that note in his suitcase? *Remember Jane. Fuck! Remember Paul. Remember Daniel Scott. Remember Warren Holden.* Was he a target? As far as he could figure, no one except George knew he was back in New York. But he still knew nothing, except that keeping God-knows-what a secret was apparently more important than a lot of innocent lives.

*

The phone's ring startled Bill awake.

"Hello."

"Good afternoon, Mr. Sanders. We have an envelope for you at the front desk. Shall I send it up to your room?"

"Who? Oh, yeah ... wait ... yes, please send it up."

"Right away."

Bill went to the bathroom and splashed some cold water on his face and thought about changing into a less wrinkled shirt, one he hadn't fallen asleep in. But after a second look in the mirror he decided the one he had on was good enough.

When he heard a knock on the door, Bill pulled a five-dollar bill out of his wallet. He opened the door, exchanged the tip for the envelope, and thanked the bellman.

The door was no sooner shut than Bill ripped open the manila envelope. The stiff Federal Express envelope inside was addressed to him at Eastside Towers. Warren Holden's office address in Santa Fe was in the sender's portion of the address form.

Inside was a single sheet of Holden's letterhead stationery. In the center was a name, in handwritten block letters: COL. (RET.) RICHARD WEST.

CHAPTER 20

Bill spent the rest of the afternoon at the main branch of the New York Public Library on Fifth Avenue. The first thing he did was search for information on Colonel Richard West. There wasn't much, and it was oddly scattered among various books, documents and websites. Born in Chicago. Worked in military intelligence for several years. Some overseas tours early on. Spent most of his career in the Pentagon. Was assigned to NATO in Brussels for five years before he retired at sixty-three. Would be seventy-three in October. No mention of family. No address listed anywhere. Otherwise, nothing seemed out of the ordinary about the guy.

What did Warren Holden mean by just giving me that name on a piece of paper? That I should contact him? What about? There's nothing obvious in his background that would link him to UFOs. Or to Paul or Cindy or Daniel Scott or events in Jefferson. Was it some kind of warning?

He also started compiling a list of what he hoped were reasonably reputable books and websites on unidentified flying objects and related unexplained phenomena.

Before heading to the library, Bill had called Sharon to apologize for his abrupt departure from Jefferson. He told her he had been called back to New York suddenly because his publisher wanted some last-minute changes in *Look Down*. He didn't want to upset her any more than she already was.

"If you need anything, just give me a call. I should have a new cell phone later today, but the number's the same. Anything new on Cindy?"

"No. Dave Taylor and the state police are still looking for

her. But now they've got Daniel Scott's murder to deal with. They keep saying they think she's a runaway. I didn't think so at first, but now I'm beginning to wonder. If she is on the run somewhere, or if she's been kidnapped, does she even know that Paul is dead? Or is she dead? My God, she's been gone for weeks."

Sharon started to choke up. Bill was on the verge of suggesting they talk about what they both knew and thought the other didn't. *No, the time's not right. That discussion needs to be face to face.*

Sharon coughed and composed herself.

"Thank you for everything, Bill. I know your being here meant a lot to Paul."

"Thanks. And remember to call if you need anything. I can easily fly back out there."

"Okay. Bye."

"Bye."

By late afternoon Bill was exhausted from lack of sleep. He also realized he hadn't eaten anything since breakfast. The stiff library chair was giving him a backache. On his way back to the Algonquin, he stopped at an AT&T store and bought a new cell phone. The sales clerk convinced him to buy a smart phone and showed him the basics of using it.

"Will phone messages and missed calls that have come in since my old phone was broken show up on this one?" Bill asked.

"Sure. Those missed calls are linked to your phone number, not the phone itself. Look, all you do is ...."

The salesman had to explain the process twice before Bill was confident he could retrieve his messages.

Back in his room, Bill fumbled through the procedure for a third time and up popped seven voice mails. Five weren't important; two were from Nancy Luke, but he had talked to her since she left them.

He then looked at missed calls that left no voice mails. There were three from Warren Holden on the day he was found dead in a Santa Fe parking garage.

Bill ordered medium-rare lamb chops and a bottle of Cabernet Sauvignon from room service. He was asleep by seven.

*

The next morning Bill woke up feeling oddly optimistic and a little chagrined at his efforts to hide. If people with helicopters at their disposal were after him, his amateur efforts to keep his whereabouts a secret seemed silly. Jefferson and the problems there were hundreds of miles behind him.

He ate breakfast in the hotel dining room and then checked out.

By nine he was getting out of a taxi in front of Eastside Towers. In the lobby, he left his duffel and backpack with George after slipping the doorman two fifty-dollar bills.

"I'll be back in a couple of hours, George. I have to drive to New Jersey to turn in a rental car. Oh, and George, forget about what I said yesterday about my being in town a secret."

"Sure. And I'll keep you bags safe here. Don't worry. Drive safely."

Another taxi to the parking garage on Forty-Second Street and he was soon on his way through the Lincoln Tunnel to the Hertz office in Montclair.

The bus ride back to Manhattan was uneventful; by 11:30 he was in his apartment and unpacking.

His early-morning optimism faded.

I can't just walk away from this. I owe it to Paul and Sharon—and Daniel Scott—to find out what the hell is going on. I owe Warren Holden, too. He gave me a key to the mystery: Colonel Richard West. But can I unlock it?

"Bill Sanders?"

Surprised, Bill looked up from a book he was reading.

"You are Bill Sanders, aren't you?"

"Yes. Do I know you?"

"Oh, no. You don't know me. I recognized you from your picture on the book jacket of *Points South*. And from some TV interviews you've done. I love that book and have wanted to meet you ever since I read it. I walk into the library today and here you are. My name is Morgen Remley. That's Morgen with an 'e.'"

She extended her right hand. Bill stood up and shook it. Her left forearm was in a cast. "I had a bicycle accident last month," she explained, lowering her voice to a whisper as a man at the next table gave her an annoyed glance. "Cast comes off day after tomorrow."

"There's a lounge just down the hall where we can talk," Bill said

Morgen Remley was a tall blonde, big-boned and athletic. She wore blue jeans, a yellow T-shirt, and sneakers. She had a small daypack slung over one shoulder. As they walked to the lounge, Bill realized how attractive she was. *Beautiful blue eyes. Probably thirty.*

They settled down in two empty chairs in a far corner of the lounge.

"So, what do you do, Morgen Remley?"

"Well, I'm an underemployed academic. I have a doctorate in marine biology, and all I've ever wanted to do is teach. Best I can do right now is a couple of adjunct jobs. But my resume is all over the East Coast. A full-time job should turn up some time, I hope. In the meantime, I'm looking for another adjunct position or some other part-time job. I don't have anything lined up for the summer yet."

Soon Morgen turned the conversation toward Bill, with deep and complex questions about *Points South* that caught Bill a bit off guard.

"You really did read that book."

"Twice. Like I said, I loved it."

She also asked Bill some personal questions about his work habits and where he grew up. She was disarmingly honest and direct. Bill responded honestly and directly.

She never mentioned Jane and neither did Bill.

After an hour, Morgen thanked Bill and said she had to leave to teach her last class for the semester at New York University.

Bill handed her his business card.

"If I can be of any help, give me a call."

"I don't have a card, but here." She scribbled her phone number on a piece of paper and handed it to him.

"Can I ask you one final question?"

"Sure."

"When I walked up to you in the reading room, I couldn't help but notice that you were reading a book on UFOs. Why?"

"Just curious. I was talking to a friend of mine about them recently. He's convinced they're real. I just wanted to see what the fuss was all about."

"That's funny because I'm sort of into UFOs myself. I'm a part-time volunteer researcher for MUFON. That's the Mutual UFO Network."

"Why would an academic be interested in something so 'out there' as UFOs? Aren't you afraid it could hurt your academic reputation? Do you keep it a secret?"

"Well, not exactly a secret. But it's true that I don't list it on teaching applications. But I think people are more open to the subject than you might think. Especially with all the recent discoveries of Earth-like planets in our Milky Way galaxy. Plus, I've always been interested in exotic life forms, which is what drew me to marine biology. What could be more exotic than extraterrestrials?"

She suddenly looked at her watch.

"Well, thanks for talking to me. I've got to run."

As Bill watched Morgen walk away, he remembered that MUFON had sent people to Jefferson to investigate the rash of UFO sightings. He also remembered Warren Holden's warning to avoid the UFO crowd.

✳

The first thing Bill did after Morgen Remley left was to head for a library computer and check her out. She was thirty-one and indeed held a doctorate in marine biology. From the University of Southern California, no less. Bachelor's and master's degrees from the University of Miami. She was listed as an adjunct assistant professor on NYU's website. He could find no mention of her work for MUFON. Probably because she was a part-time volunteer. Or maybe she didn't want her name publicly listed with the group.

But I'm still a little suspicious. This seems a little too coincidental. A woman introduces herself to me and she just happens to be a part-time UFO researcher. What the hell does that mean? I'm up to my neck in UFOs. But how could she know I was in the library? Or did she? Maybe what I've been going through has made me a little paranoid. Maybe I've always been that way. Jane used to chide me for being secretive. She said I was too much of a loner. Maybe I need to trust somebody. Morgen Remley?

✳

That evening he called Dave Taylor at his home in Jefferson.

"Dave, it's Bill Sanders. Sorry to bother you at home."

"That's okay. It's part of my job."

"I just wanted to check to see if there was anything new on Cindy Watson or Daniel Scott. I'm back in New York. I had to leave Jefferson suddenly."

"Yeah, I know. Sharon said you had a book crisis or something."

"It's under control now."

"Well, there's nothing new here. Cindy is still missing. The Daniel Scott murder is a doozey. The state police say they have never seen a murder case so lacking in clues. I'm not sure it'll ever be solved. Poor guy. You got anything you want to tell me? Remember our agreement?"

"Of course. But I don't know anything you don't." *Except the note I found in my duffel and the map I stole from Daniel Scott's room.* "Did you ever talk to that farmer, Mr. Baker, who said he saw a helicopter just before Paul's crash?"

"No. That's a waste of time. Just drop it."

"I guess you're right. Well, I probably won't be coming back to Jefferson anytime soon unless Sharon asks me to. Thanks for your help."

"Thanks for yours. Hell, if it weren't for you, we would still be thinking Daniel was a suicide. Sorry I got a little testy about helicopters and that UFO stuff."

"No problem. I may call back in a week or so if that's okay with you."

Sure ... oh, wait a second. I just remembered. There is one odd little thing. When we got around to searching Daniel Scott's room at the Wayne Hotel late that afternoon, his key was missing from its box behind the front desk. Mrs. Wayne said he always put the key in the box when he left. It wasn't with his wallet and other stuff found in his pockets. But here's the strange thing. Mrs. Wayne called the next day to say that the key was delivered with the mail. Don't know what to make of that."

"That is strange. Was anything missing from his room?"

"No way to tell because we didn't know what was there to start with. Everything seemed in order. If somebody was in that room, they weren't looking to steal stuff. His fancy laptop was there, plugged in and running. None of his files looked like they had been disturbed."

"Any fingerprints?"

"Just Daniel's and the cleaning lady's. Prints on the keys were too smudged to even bother with."

"Maybe Daniel did take his key with him that once and accidently dropped it somewhere before he was killed. A stranger could have found it and dropped it in a mailbox."

"That's as good an explanation as any. We'll probably never know. Well, take care."

"You, too. Bye."

Bill realized he was sweating when he tapped off his cell. The woman he encountered at the Wayne Hotel—apparently Mrs. Wayne—obviously didn't know who he was or make any connection between him and the missing key. She went into a back room before he made the call to the Sheriff from her pay phone. She must have heard nothing, or she would have told Dave about a strange man calling his office.

I've got to come clean with Dave. But not yet.

The next few days Bill holed up in his apartment, searching the Internet and skim-reading library books and some books he bought from Barnes & Noble on UFOs. He was thoroughly confused as to what, if anything, to take seriously and what to ignore. Or whether he was wasting his time. UFO sites on the Internet were even more bizarre and confusing. One thing that caught Bill's attention were occasional references to big triangular craft like Paul and those Jefferson kids described. He needed help and someone to talk to. *But everyone I know would laugh at the first mention of UFOs.*

Finally, he searched through his wallet and found the piece of paper with Morgen Remley's number scribbled on it. *Maybe she can help me. She said she was a UFO researcher. At least she won't think I'm crazy. Besides, I like her. I like her name. Morgen. German for morning.*

CHAPTER 21

"Morgen Remley?"

"Yes."

"It's Bill Sanders."

"Oh. Gosh. What a surprise."

"I was wondering. Did you find a summer job?"

"No, but I'm looking hard."

"Well, how about having lunch with me tomorrow. I have an idea that might interest you."

"Sure. That'd be great. When and where?"

"Where do you live?"

"In Brooklyn. Carroll Gardens."

"Do you like Japanese food?"

"Love it!"

"How about the Sushi Palace just off Washington Square near NYU? Do you know it?"

"Yes, I've eaten there a couple of times before. It's great."

"Good. I like it, too. See you there tomorrow. Is one okay?"

"Perfect."

"See you then. Bye."

"Bye."

Bill's apartment was on the thirty-second floor and the south window of his living room allowed a commanding view of the East River and the United Nations building.

After his short conversation with Morgen, Bill stood at the window for a few minutes staring into space, doubts again nagging at him. *I ought to drop this whole mess. What can I do that the police can't? Nothing can bring back Paul, Daniel Scott, or Warren Holden. What am I looking for? Helicopters and UFOs? Based on what? A missing child, an alcoholic friend's weird story, three deaths that may be totally unrelated, A half-blind farmer, a dying friend's last word, a night watchman who saw some lights in the sky that were probably airplanes, a map with a bunch of Xs and 0s that may mean nothing, a retired colonel with no home address?*

But as this improbable list formed in his mind, Bill knew he couldn't walk away. The improbable list was just too improbable. And what about the threat in the note he found in his duffel after the break-in at Paul's? The dots must connect. He couldn't let it go. Then there were Paul's pleas to him: *I'm afraid. I don't have many friends left. You're the only person who can help me ... Do you really think I would bring you out here to lie to you? Have we ever lied to each other? I know what I saw. And if you won't believe me, or at least hear me out, then I'm lost. I have nowhere to turn ... Help me.*

Bill had promised to help. Paul was beyond help now, but Cindy was still missing. Bill knew he would keep his promise to Paul. His promise to himself. Now he wanted to know the truth. His reporter's instincts were stirring after two years of submission to fiction.

The apartment phone's ringing broke his concentration.

"Hello."

"Bill, it's Nancy. Are you okay?"

"Sure. Why wouldn't I be?"

"Well, a friend of mind said she saw you at the Algonquin Hotel. So, I knew you were back in town last week. I just wondered why you hadn't called."

"Nancy, I'm sorry. I've just been so involved in my friend's death and helping his wife that I haven't had time to think about anything else. How about we have lunch Wednesday at Dave's?"

"Sounds good. We have some business to discuss, but it can wait until then."

"Great. Wednesday then."

"Okay. Bye."

*

Bill and Morgen both ordered the sushi lunch special with miso soup and salad.

Morgen wore jeans, T-shirt and sneakers again, only these jeans were white, and the shirt was green with an NYU logo on its front. Her long blond hair was pulled back in a retro ponytail, which accentuated her intense blue eyes.

Bill questioned Morgen about her job search.

"Well, it seems there's too much competition for the jobs I'm really qualified for. For other jobs I'm willing to take, especially for the summer, I'm overqualified. That frightens some people. I've been thinking of putting together a second CV that leaves out my advanced degrees."

"This may be a nosy question, but how are you able to get along in a place like New York with so little income?"

"My parents were killed in a car wreck when I was nine. They had no money or life insurance. An uncle in Kansas raised me and helped pay my college expenses. He died about five years ago. He left me what little money he had, and I've been super careful with it. I manage. I also have a roommate, which helps."

Male or female? Now that is nosy.

The waiter brought the soup.

By the time the sushi arrived, Morgen was asking the questions.

"You said you had an idea that might interest me. What's up?"

"I need a research assistant for a month, maybe two. Would you be interested?"

"What kind of research? Are you working on another book?"

"No. It's personal. I'm trying to find a missing girl. It's complicated."

"What's it got to do with marine biology?"

"Nothing."

"Then why me?"

Bill paused, dipped a piece of raw salmon into some soy sauce, and looked directly at Morgen.

"Because of your interest in UFOs. You told me last week that you were 'sort of' into UFOs, that you were a volunteer researcher for MUFON."

"Was the missing girl abducted?"

"Maybe. I don't know."

"You're pretty vague about all this. I'm not sure what you want me to do."

Do I trust my instincts and take a chance on her? I need someone to know everything I know, but who is not as personally involved as I am. Someone who can be more objective. Who can help connect the dots. I don't know anyone else who will take me seriously if I mention UFOs.

"I said this was complicated. You have no idea how complicated. Let's finish lunch and take a walk. I'll tell you everything. If you want to walk away, fine. You just have to swear that if you turn down my offer, everything I tell you is confidential. Between just the two of us. No MUFON. No notes. No nothing."

"That's fair."

For the next two hours Bill and Morgen talked as they walked around the NYU campus on a warm late spring afternoon. Bill told her everything. Paul's drinking. The UFO sightings by Paul and others. The threatening note in his bag. The map he took from Daniel Scott's room. The truck fires that blocked the bridge. All his conversations with Paul and Dave Taylor. And Warren Holden. The mysterious Colonel West. Everything.

"But your friend is dead. The police are looking for his daughter. A lot of what happened could be coincidence. You may be heading down a rabbit hole. There may never be answers. Why not just drop it?"

"Believe me, I've been tempted. But I made a promise to Paul to do everything I could to find his daughter. I can't just give up on that. Was I in some way responsible for the deaths of Daniel Scott and Warren Holden? What about the UFO stuff? And don't forget the threat to me. There's a web, a pattern. I just have to figure it out. I need your help. I can pay you well. Money is not an issue."

"Can I think about this overnight and call you tomorrow morning?"

"I guess that's fair, too. Call my cell. About nine."

Am I doing the right thing? I like her. I want to trust her.

✳

That night he dreamed again of trying to stop Jane from boarding the Air France flight. But he awoke in less of a panic than usual and was able to go right back to sleep.

Bill was on his third cup of coffee and reading the Times when his cell phone started chirping. *I've got to figure out how to change that ring tone.*

"Hello."

"Bill, it's Morgen."

"How are you this morning?"

"Well, I didn't get much sleep last night. Everything you told me kept running through my head like a movie on a loop. Over and over."

"Did you make a decision?"

"Yes. I'll do it. But we need to talk about the details."

"Can you come over to my apartment?"

"Yes. Is around eleven good? What's the address?"

"That's fine. I'm in Eastside Towers on East Seventy-Second Street. Between Lexington and Third. Apartment 32-B."

"That's the high rent district. Will they let a poor girl like me in that neighborhood?"

"Ask for George in the lobby. He'll take care of you."

"Okay. See you in a couple of hours."

*

Morgen was wearing tan slacks and a red blouse when she rang Bill's doorbell. Her hair was pulled into a stylish twist on top of her head.

"Come in. Welcome," Bill said as he opened the door. "How about some coffee before we talk?"

"That would be great. But could I have tea?"

Morgen marveled at the view from the apartment. The living room was bigger than her entire apartment in Brooklyn. The galley kitchen was next to a dining alcove. There were two bedrooms; one Bill used for an office. The decor was eclectic. Nothing matched, but it all seemed to work together.

"This is quite a place."

"Thanks. My wife picked it out."

"I'm sorry."

"No. No. That's fine. Sit. Let's talk."

Bill directed Morgen to a club chair; he sat in a wingback chair facing her at a forty-five-degree angle. She was wearing a light musky perfume he liked.

"Let's get the money details settled first. I propose to pay you a thousand dollars a week, four weeks guaranteed with an option for four more at my discretion. There may be some travel. I'll pay all the expenses. Hours will be irregular. Will that work for you?"

"Yes. It's very generous."

"When can you start?"

"How about tomorrow morning?"

"Perfect. Any questions?"

"Not a question really, just a comment. The first thing I want to do tomorrow is have you go over the whole series of events again, in as much detail as you can, while I take notes. I want to hear as much detail as possible."

"We can do that. Then we can make some plans about how to proceed. Where are we going to start? With Colonel West?"

"Maybe. Seems logical. That's where your politician friend pointed you."

Morgen asked if she could have a glass of water, which Bill brought from the kitchen.

"I have an idea," he said. "It's after noon. How about lunch? There's a good Italian place just two blocks away."

"Good idea. I'm hungry. I didn't have any breakfast."

*

Morgen showed up at ten the next morning. Her daypack was filled with notebooks and a digital voice recorder.

They settled down in the same chairs they had sat in the day before.

"I hope you don't mind if I record this. I'm also going to take notes. When I go over the notes I want to listen to the recording at the same time. It may help me pick up things I missed. Plus, when I hear my questions again, I may think of others I should have asked."

"Whatever works."

For the next five hours Bill recounted in minute detail his experiences of the past few weeks, beginning with the call for help from Paul and ending with meeting Morgen in the library. He left nothing out.

Morgen's questions were sharp and probing, often psychological in nature. She often wanted to know how Bill felt about an event or a person. Did he think an action or event was right or wrong, good or bad? She was especially intrigued by the account of Sam Wiggins, the security guard who told Bill and Paul he saw shafts of strange lights at night and heard the sounds of helicopters.

"Do you think he was telling the truth?"

"Well, yeah. Why would he lie? He didn't seem like the type."

She was also extremely interested in every detail of Paul's description to Bill of the craft that held Cindy in the blue light.

"You're sure she was being put back into her room, not taken from it?"

"That's what Paul said."

"How significant a factor do you think his drinking was?"

"A lot, I guess. Especially later. It may have killed him. But I don't think it affected what he saw the night Cindy disappeared. I was doubtful at first, but I have come to believe that he saw what he said he saw. Whatever that was."

CHAPTER 22

Bill and Morgen agreed they should begin by searching for Colonel Richard West and any connection between him and events in Jefferson.

It was a rainy Saturday afternoon; they were sitting at Bill's dining table going over notes, looking for loose ends and clues they might have missed.

"I have a couple of good sources from my reporting days who I think are still at the Pentagon. I'll try to contact them Monday and see if I can get any leads on West. If nothing else maybe they can trace him by finding out where his pension is mailed or deposited.

"But before we get into hunting for West, I need your help. I've been skim-reading all this UFO stuff in books and on the Internet, and I'm confused. I'm not sure what's important and what's baloney. I just don't have enough background knowledge to be able to focus on what might be real and ignore the rest."

"Can you summarize what you're read about so far?"

"Well, the main thing I've picked up so far is that UFO researchers and a lot of other people are convinced governments, especially ours, know much more about UFOs and extraterrestrials than they are letting on. The researchers think governments are waging a massive disinformation campaign to make them and those who claim to have seen UFOs or have been abducted by aliens look like a bunch of weirdos. Not a hard job given some of the accounts of witnesses and abductees I've read. It also seems to be working, given Dave Taylor's reaction to the subject."

"True enough. But tell me about the cases you've read about."

Bill recounted tales of the concealment of ancient artifacts that prove advanced civilizations have visited Earth for thousands of years; of theories that structures like the pyramids of Giza were built by or with the help of aliens; of aliens coming not only from other galaxies but from other dimensions or universes, or from the future; of alien-human breeding programs; of livestock mutilations; of UFOs powered by antigravity engines; of crop circles and government efforts to make the circles appear to be hoaxes; of crashed UFOs and dead aliens kept in a secret base in Nevada; of a secret treaty between extraterrestrials and the U.S. government that allows the aliens to abduct and do experiments on humans in exchange for technology; of UFO bases on Mars and the moon that NASA has photographed and kept secret; of American and Russian spacecraft destroyed by UFOs; of people who have died mysteriously or disappeared while investigating the cover-up of UFOs.

"Well, you've certainly covered a lot of ground. That may be the problem. You're not really making a distinction between the highly improbable, obviously ridiculous, and the credible. You need to concentrate on a small number of specific cases that are the most credible and give you a more focused look at what may be going on. Also, always remember that UFO stands for unidentified flying object. But just because an object in the sky can't be identified doesn't mean it's from outer space. Most UFO sightings have very conventional explanations. It's the very few that can't be explained easily that interest MUFON and me. These are the one you should zero in on.

"How about at home tonight I compile a list of what I think are the half dozen or so cases you should study in depth? I'll e-mail it to you either later tonight or early in the morning. You can work on them tomorrow. Everything you need is on the Internet. Then on Monday we'll go after Colonel Richard West, who could be hiding in plain sight for all we know."

"That sounds good. I'll look for your e-mail, do more reading tomorrow and see you back here Monday at nine sharp." *I feel like I've just had a college lecture and a homework assignment. Is it my imagination, or has Morgen's tone turned a bit bossy? Guess it's the teacher in her.*

✳

Bill checked his e-mail at about ten, just before going to bed. Nothing.

As he was drifting off, Morgen's comment about Colonel West "hiding in plain sight" popped into his head. *What the hell did she mean by that? Maybe nothing. Maybe she meant that finding him would be easy. Just because information about him is scarce didn't mean he's hiding. After all, the only place I've looked for him so far is the New York Public Library.*

✳

Bill awoke at seven. The rain had moved on and the morning was clear and fresh. The first thing he did was to go into his office and check his e-mail. There was a message from Morgen. It had come in at one-thirty. He decided not to open it until he took a shower and had some coffee.

Thirty minutes later he was back at his computer, printing Morgen's e-mail. It was simple and to the point: a list of six events for him to research. He only glanced at them briefly before focusing on a short note Morgen added explaining the events were listed in chronological order, not in order of importance. "There are two kinds of important," she wrote. "First, important to the overall field of UFO research and, second, important to the events you encountered in Indiana. After you read up on these cases, let's try to rank them in terms of the second. See you at nine tomorrow. M."

Bill took a longer look at the list:

1. Roswell UFO crash – 1947
2. Rendlesham Forest incident – 1980

3. Hudson Valley sightings – 1983 to 1986.
4. Belgian UFO wave – 1989 to 1990
5. Pine Bush sightings – 1990 to present
6. Phoenix lights – 1997

The only ones on the list he recognized were the Roswell crash and the Phoenix lights. He'd come across both in his recent research but didn't read much about them since he didn't grasp their importance. He also remembered watching part of a television documentary years ago on Roswell. Something about a crashed flying saucer in New Mexico, alien bodies, and a military cover-up. He remembered even less about the Phoenix lights: just an image of a newspaper photo of some lights in the sky. *Homework to do.*

Bill did a Google search on Roswell and UFO and more than three-quarters of a million hits popped up. He looked through the first fifteen or so and picked three that looked serious and to the point. He printed them out. He did the same for the other five cases. He hated reading documents on a computer screen.

Bill put the stack of printouts, a yellow legal pad, and two mechanical pencils on his coffee table in the living room before going to the kitchen for another cup of coffee. He then settled down in the living room club chair, which still smelled faintly of Morgen's perfume, and started reading about the cases in the order Morgen listed them, beginning with Roswell. After reading about each case, he wrote a short summary of it.

In July 1947, the public information officer at Roswell Army Air Field in Roswell, New Mexico, issued a press release that the military had recovered a "flying disc" that crashed on a nearby ranch. The Army soon retracted the press release, saying instead that what was recovered was only a weather balloon. The story quickly faded.

Interest in the Roswell incident was reignited thirty years later when UFO researchers started interviewing people with connections to the event. The conclusions drawn from these witnesses were that an alien spacecraft crashed in a thunderstorm, extraterrestrial bodies were recovered, and a massive government cover-up ensued. Several books about Roswell prompted congressional inquiries and an Air Force internal investigation. The Air Force concluded what was recovered at Roswell was not a weather balloon but debris from Project Mogul, a military surveillance project using high-altitude balloons. The bodies were explained as life-like dummies used to test how pilots might survive falls from high altitudes. Researchers scoffed at these explanations as outlandish disinformation, pointing out that the tests with the dummies didn't take place until the 1950s, years after the Roswell incident.

An interesting side story to Roswell was the emergence of Majestic 12 in 1984. Majestic 12 is supposedly the code name for a secret group put together by President Harry Truman in the aftermath of Roswell to deal with, and manage the cover-up of, the UFO phenomenon. According to UFO lore, the group is still in existence today. Majestic 12 came to light when a top-secret document was reportedly leaked to a UFO researcher. The FBI said the document was a fake.

Bill suddenly remembered standing in a cold Kentucky cornfield staring at the midnight sky with a group of people who swore they saw UFOs in the area the night before. The only thing he saw that night was his frosty breath and bright stars. That was almost 30 years ago when a state editor assigned him to the story. That was the only time until his recent trip to Jefferson that he had ever given a serious thought to UFOs, and he'd completely forgotten it until now.

He shuffled the printouts and pulled out the ones dealing with Rendlesham Forest.

Located in Suffolk near RAF Woodbridge and Bentwaters military bases, Rendlesham Forest was the scene in December 1980 of the most famous and intriguing UFO case in Britain. The U.S. Air Force was using the base at the time.

At around three o'clock in the morning of December 26, a U.S. security patrol headed into Rendlesham Forest to investigate strange lights that were thought to be a downed aircraft. What they found was a strange, glowing metallic object with colored lights. As they approached the object, animals on a nearby farm went into a frenzy. One of the servicemen described the object as a "craft of unknown origin" that felt warm when he touched it. He also said the craft had symbols on its body, which he copied. The object then flew away.

Over the next two days and nights local police and military personnel investigated the area. Plaster casts were taken of imprints thought to have been left by the object's landing gear. During these investigations, flashing lights were seen in a nearby field and other lights were seen in the sky.

Years later the serviceman who touched the craft agreed to undergo regression hypnosis. While hypnotized, he claimed the craft came from the future and was occupied by time travelers, not extraterrestrials. Other witnesses later described the craft as small and triangular shaped.

The Rendlesham Forest incident is important in the annals of UFO sightings because of the credibility of the witnesses. The base commander aided in the investigation.

Bill stood up and walked into the kitchen for another cup of coffee. He wondered what researchers would think of Paul's credibility.

He settled back into his chair. The Hudson Valley sightings were next.

Between 1983 and 1986 there were scores of UFO sightings in the historic Hudson River Valley north of New York City. Hundreds of eyewitnesses described the craft they saw as huge, silent, and triangular-shaped.

One account by a computer engineer who was driving home late at night was typical: "Out of nowhere, I got a lot of static on the radio. I thought maybe I was on the wrong number, and then I turned the dial again and that's when I looked up and saw this craft. It was a triangular ship. And the back had to be as large as a football field at least. And there was no noise."

The computer engineer pulled off the highway and joined a group of motorists who were looking at the craft he had seen from his car. It continued moving north over the Hudson Valley. More and more people saw it, including a police officer who described it as four hundred yards wide.

There were later charges that the sightings were a hoax perpetuated by private pilots flying their small planes in formation. Most witnesses and experts rejected this explanation.

A number of books were written about the Hudson Valley sightings. Perhaps the best known is "Night Siege: The Hudson Valley UFO Sightings," by Dr. J. Allen Hynek, Philip J. Imbrogno, and Bob Pratt. Dr. Hynek was an astronomer who originally was hired by the U.S. government to investigate and debunk UFO sightings. In the course of many investigations, he switched sides and concluded that many eyewitness accounts were genuine. Dr. Hynek also developed the "close encounters" classification system to describe UFO events, which helped earn him a cameo in the movie "Close Encounters of the Third Kind."

Bill reread his Hudson Valley summary. He felt a chill on the back of his neck, just as he did when he'd read the printouts earlier. He recalled Paul's words: *When my eyes adjusted a little to the brightness, I looked up and that's when I saw it. A big goddamn machine, shaped like a triangle, bigger than the house and the clearing, was just hanging there in the sky about a hundred feet over the roof. I again thought it must be a helicopter, but it was too big and there was still no sound. It was absolutely silent.* Bill also remembered The Jefferson Courier story about the two teenagers who claimed to have seen a UFO. They described it as triangular-shaped and bigger than a barn. Earlier stories Sarah Wong gave him had similar descriptions by witnesses.

He leaned back in the chair and closed his eyes. *Is this what Morgen meant by ranking these cases in terms of their importance to events in Jefferson? Are big, triangular craft the link between the Hudson Valley sightings and Cindy's disappearance? What about the Rendlesham Forest craft? It was triangular but small. Maybe a little bigger than a car?*

Bill stood up to stretch and take a break. An electronic chirp from the computer in his office told him he had a new e-mail.

It was from Morgen: "Bill: There's a seventh case I think you should take a look at. It's the Travis Walton abduction in 1975. Lots of stuff about it on the web. Hope you're having fun. See you tomorrow. M."

Since it was too late to consider the Travis Walton case in chronological order, Bill decided to save it until last.

He turned to the Belgian UFO wave of 1989 and 1990.

A wave, also sometimes called a flap, is UFO-speak for a cluster of sightings. That was certainly the case in Belgium between November 1989 and April 1990. During that period, thousands of people, including at least three groups of police officers, reported seeing large, triangular-shaped objects moving slowly at low altitudes over the Belgian countryside. One of the objects was picked up on NATO radar and chased by two Belgian Air Force F-16 jet fighters. Radar images showed the object dropping almost two miles in five seconds!

A dramatic photo taken by a witness showed the underbelly of a black, triangular craft with a light in the center and three lights at the corners of the triangle.

The Belgian Air Force and government officials cooperated fully with the press and UFO investigators, releasing everything related to the sightings, including tapes of the craft as they were picked up on radar. Although there were thousands of sightings in Belgium, there were only a few in the neighboring countries of Germany, France, the Netherlands, and Luxembourg.

No one has been able to explain the Belgian wave, which ended after a few months. Skeptics blame the entire series of events on mass hysteria. Witnesses say this is laughable, especially in light of radar data and the credibility of many witnesses.

Bill put his pencil down and studied a copy of the photograph of the Belgian UFO. *I'm no expert, but this sure looks real to me. Is this what Paul saw?*

Bill sighed and started reading the printouts of the Pine Bush sightings.

Pine Bush, a small town in Orange County with a population of a few thousand people, is about 85 miles northwest of New York City and thirty-five miles northwest of West Point and the Hudson River. Pine Bush is linked, at least geographically, to the Hudson Valley sightings.

For almost a century strange objects and lights have been reported in and around Pine Bush. But it was in the late 1980s and early 1990s that the town became a UFO hot spot, attracting national attention. That was due to an increased number of sightings and a 1991book, "Silent Invasion: The Shocking Discoveries of a UFO Researcher," by

Ellen Crystal.

Crystal's book about sightings by her and others of strange craft and extraterrestrial creatures in and around Pine Bush caused a sensation and turned the town into a magnet for the media and UFO hunters. It was as though the Hudson Valley sightings of a few years earlier had reappeared a few miles to the west. Except that the Pine Bush UFOs were more varied in size and shape. They included large, triangular-shaped craft like the ones seen in the Hudson Valley, as well as some large ones that were boomerang-shaped. Others were much smaller and described as globe-like or saucer-shaped.

But the big difference between the Pine Bush and Hudson Valley events was the sightings of alien beings, which Crystal claimed to have photographed. Her book included several photos, which critics said were blurry and inconclusive. The aliens were described as having thin reptilian bodies and large yellow eyes. Most people who claim to have encountered aliens have described them as "grays," small humanoid creatures with gray skin, large hairless heads, and dark, almond-shaped eyes. This was the description of the bodies reportedly recovered in Roswell.

Skeptics of the Pine Bush sighting said people were simply seeing conventional aircraft from nearby airports, including a military airfield in nearby Newburgh. Witnesses scoffed at this explanation, pointing to many photographs and videos of objects that appeared to be incompatible with conventional planes. Also, during sightings, researchers often checked with the control towers at nearby airports. Most of the time the towers reported no aircraft in the area.

UFO sightings in Pine Bush slowed to a trickle by the end of the 1990s, as locals grew tired of visitors gathering along roads in fields at night. Plus, the town was growing and many of the favorite areas for viewing were turning into subdivisions.

Bill suddenly realized he was hungry. He pushed the printouts and his notes aside and headed for the kitchen. A few minutes later he was having a roast beef sandwich and a glass of milk in the dining alcove. He could see the United Nations building from where he sat. *If these UFOs and aliens are real—and that's a big if for me—then why all the secrecy and intrigue? Why don't they just land at the UN or the White House and announce themselves? What are their intentions? A lot of UFO researchers think they are trying to help us. If they were hostile, wouldn't they have done something to harm us already?*

Then he remembered something he read years ago about the European conquest of the Americas. *When advanced civilizations make contact with primitive civilizations, it never goes well for the latter.*

Bill finished his sandwich and milk, put the dish and glass into the dishwasher, and settled back into his club chair. He had two more cases to go: the Phoenix lights and Travis Walton.

The Phoenix lights case was a mass UFO sighting witnessed and reported by thousands of people, including the governor of Arizona, on the night of March 13, 1997.

There were actually two groups of lights. The first was seen over a wide area of the state, from its border with Nevada, through the Phoenix area, and south to the edge of Tucson. The second was a series of stationary lights in the Phoenix area. The Air Force identified the second group as flares that were being dropped in a training exercise.

It was the first group of lights that couldn't be easily explained.

Witnesses not only reported seeing lights but also the structure of a wedge-shaped craft that was described as huge, as big as two or three football fields. As the craft passed slowly overhead, it blocked out the stars behind it. One witness said it made a sound like "rushing wind." Most said it was silent.

It was unclear whether there was one craft or several.

Kurt Russell, the move star, told the BBC years later that he was flying his private plane into Phoenix that March night in 1997 when he spotted the lights. He said he reported the sighting to the control tower at Sky Harbor International Airport.

Skeptics say the lights were nothing more than some small planes flying in formation: a hoax, in other words. But hundreds of photographs and videos of the lights cast doubt on this explanation, according to witnesses and UFO researchers. They also point to the lights' silence, which would be highly unlikely for a group of planes. And, they argue, what about people who say the craft blocked out stars when it passed overhead? Finally, they point to the large number of highly credible witnesses, including police officers, pilots, and even the governor.

Bill stopped writing, leaned his head back, and closed his eyes. *This was the fourth case in which the UFOs more or less resembled what Paul said he saw. What about the others? Do UFOs come in different sizes and models? Are we being visited by extraterrestrials from different places that look different and have different craft? Why would they all be so interested in us?*

Bill suddenly realized his questions assumed the reality of UFOs and alien beings. *Probably from reading about these convincing and unexplained cases. Was that Morgen's plan? To convert me? Or am I becoming a victim of the J. Allen Hynek Syndrome: study something you're skeptical about long enough and you come to accept it.*

The Travis Walton abduction case. Bill shifted in his chair and realized he hadn't printed out any information.

In his office he Googled "Travis Walton abduction" and got almost two hundred thousand hits. As with the other cases, he picked what he thought were the best three from the top fifteen and printed them out. He read them while still sitting at his desk. He returned to his living room chair and picked up his legal pad and a pencil. He kept thinking of Cindy. He fought back bile and forced himself to concentrate.

Travis Walton was a logger from Snowflake, Arizona, who was working with a crew of six other loggers in the Apache-Sitgreaves National Forest on November 5, 1975.

After a day of work, the men were returning home in a pickup truck when they said they came upon a luminous, saucer-shaped object hovering over the ground about a hundred feet away. Despite warnings from his companions, Walton got out of the truck to get a closer look at the object. As he looked up at the object he was struck by a beam of blue light and knocked to the ground.

Walton's companions, panic-stricken, sped away in their truck. However, they shortly turned the truck around and returned to help him. But Walton was nowhere to be found. The saucer-like object was also gone.

The men drove into Snowflake and recounted their story to police.

A massive search for Walton began amid concerns that he might be injured and unable to survive the cold nights. Still there were no signs of him. Police began to suspect foul play and started looking for bad blood between Walton and members of the crew. All six took polygraph tests. Five passed; one was inconclusive. Investigations decided there was no reason to suspect murder.

Five days after Walton disappeared, he returned. He was found at a small filling station in a nearby town. He was weak, hungry, dehydrated, and disoriented; he had lost weight. He told investigators: "Consciousness returned to me on the night I awoke to find myself on the cold pavement west of Heber, Arizona. I was lying on my stomach, my head on my right forearm. Cold air brought me instantly awake." He thought only a few hours had passed since he approached the craft and was struck by the blue light.

What happened to Travis Walton?

He later told investigators that after being thrown backwards by the blue light in the forest, he awoke to find himself on a hospital-like examining table. Three non-human creatures surrounded him. His description of them was similar to "grays" described in the Roswell case and by other abductees. The creatures' large, dark almond-shaped eyes were their most distinctive and frightening feature.

Walton said he was subjected to several medical procedures and tests.

The Walton case is one of the most compelling in UFO history. Skeptics say it was a scheme by Walton to make money, pointing to Walton's book about his encounter, "The Walton Experience," which was made into a major motion picture titled "Fire in the Sky." Others say the abduction story was made up to distract from a logging contract the men were in danger of not fulfilling.

Skeptics also say polygraphs, or lie detector tests, are not perfect. But five of the crew passed the tests in 1975; the sixth did not complete the exam. In 1993, when the film "Fire in the Sky" was released, three of the loggers agreed to take polygraph tests again. All three passed.

When Bill finished his summary of the Travis Walton case, he felt even sicker to his stomach as his thoughts returned to Cindy. He remembered Paul's words: *Cindy was floating inside that beam of blue light, in the air, between her window and the object.*

Bill forced himself to go back over parts of the Travis Walton abduction. *Walton and his crew said he was knocked to the ground by a beam of blue light. He also said he was subjected to medical procedures. What kind of medical procedures would leave him exhausted, hungry, dehydrated, underweight, and disoriented? Had something like this happened to Cindy? Maybe Paul was confused about Cindy returning to her room in the blue light. Maybe she was being taken into the craft. She was only ten years old. Did fear and trauma kill her? If she died at the hands of extraterrestrials, where's her body? Maybe these aliens and their ships aren't here to help us after all. Maybe they're not so benign. They certainly weren't kind to Travis Walton.*

CHAPTER 23

Bill got up at six on Monday morning to type his handwritten summaries of the seven cases into his computer and then print them out so Morgen wouldn't have to struggle with his handwriting.

She arrived promptly at nine.

"Coffee?"

"Mmm ... a little sugar."

"Want something to eat? Toast? Eggs?"

"No thanks. I had some cereal and bananas at home."

Coffee mug in hand, Morgen sat in the club chair. Bill settled into the sofa, facing her. He handed her his summaries.

Bill studied Morgen as she read. She was wearing that musky perfume again. Blue jeans, sneakers, and a T-shirt seemed to be her uniform. He noticed her socks didn't match. Her jeans were split over both knees. Her hair was pulled into a ponytail, held in place by a rubber band. No jewelry or makeup. Bill found himself intrigued by her. Her blue eyes were striking. He wondered if she was wearing colored contacts.

Bill took a long sip from his coffee mug just as Morgen glanced up at him.

"These summaries are good. You got the essence of each case very nicely."

"Well, I didn't spend all those years as a reporter for nothing."

"So, what do you think?"

"I found the Travis Walton abduction case the most interesting, mainly because of the lie detector tests. I know they're not one hundred percent reliable, but most of the time they're close. Six of those seven guys passed. Years later, when the movie came out, three of them took a polygraph test and passed again. That's pretty compelling. It's also the only one of the cases that involved an abduction."

"Anything else?"

"You said in your e-mail that we should rank these cases relative to their importance to what happened in Indiana."

"And?"

"Well, four of the cases—Hudson Valley, the Belgian wave, Pine Bush, and the Phoenix lights—all involved UFOs that were similar to the one described by Paul. The Belgian and Hudson Valley craft seemed closest to what he said he saw. Then we're back to Travis Walton. While the craft was not the same, Walton was struck by a blue light, which was witnessed by six people. Paul said Cindy was being transported either to or from her room in a blue light."

Morgen crossed her legs and started drawing concentric circles on the Walton summary.

"What do you think this means?"

"Damned if I know. Except maybe that Paul was telling the truth. He wouldn't make up those details. Especially the color of the light."

"But hadn't there been sightings reported in the local paper? MUFON had researchers there for a time, but they didn't really find anything."

"Yes, but I know Paul. I don't think he was influenced by those stories. And none of the stories said anything about a blue light."

"Looking at these seven cases I gave you to study, some of them contain details in common with what Paul described, right? Well, the reason I gave you those cases is that they are among the most compelling sightings and abduction events ever recorded. And you're right about Travis Walton. It's an awesome story. So are the Belgian sightings because, like some recent sightings by the U.S. military, they are backed up by radar data. These seven cases are important to the overall field of UFO research; five of them are important to Paul's case because they tend to have similarities to his account. But we're not sure what that means, if anything. I recommend that we recognize these links but put them aside for a time and concentrate on finding this Colonel West character. What's the name of the ex-senator who sent you his name?"

"Holden. Warren Holden."

"Right. He died of a heart attack in Santa Fe. And he warned you to avoid people like me."

"Yeah, but I think he meant not to get mixed up in UFO turf wars. Or with people who are too far out there. I don't think he meant you."

"That's comforting."

"Also, did Holden really die of a heart attack or was he killed? Remember, his death came on the heels of the murder of Daniel Scott. Paul's fatal crash may have resulted from being chased by a mysterious helicopter. And don't forget the truck fires on the bridge in Louisville that made me miss my flight to Atlanta."

"Strange stuff, I agree. But it was Holden himself, on the day before he died, who sent you the name of Colonel West. Holden was clearly trying to tell you something, or at least point you in the right direction. Let's go there. We agreed on Friday that would be our first move."

"You're right. But Morgen, before we start looking for Colonel West, I need your take on something."

"What?"

"I'm an old-fashioned reporter and a natural skeptic. This UFO thing is all new and very strange to me. I don't know what to think about it. But let's assume for the sake of discussion that UFOs and extraterrestrials are real. We don't seem to know what they're doing here. Maybe the government knows, but it ain't telling. So here are my questions: Are these aliens helping us or hurting us? Are they benign or hostile? Should we welcome them or prepare for war?"

"Those are good questions. There are no good answers. It depends on who you talk to."

"I'll bet Travis Walton has an opinion on this."

"Well, I don't think he would serve on a UFO welcoming committee. But for every Travis Walton there are other abductees who claim a positive experience. Some say they have been given messages from extraterrestrials that they are here to help us. By that the aliens say they mean to keep humans from destroying the earth, either by nuclear war or environmental destruction. Interestingly, a significant number of UFO sightings and abductions, including Roswell and Rendlesham Forest, have occurred near nuclear facilities. Then there are cases like your friend Paul's. Nothing apparently positive about it. A ten-year-old girl is missing. Travis Walton was returned after about five days. Cindy is still missing after more than a month. Here's what bothers me. If the aliens meant to harm us, they certainly have the technology to do it big time. But they're not doing that. They often seem indifferent to us, while at the same time very interested in us. Does that make any sense?"

"Yes ... no. I've wondered the same thing."

"This confusion about motives shows up in popular culture. Look at movies. They range from benign extraterrestrials in *Close Encounters of the Third Kind* to any number of monster-aliens-from-outer-space-try-to-destroy-Earth films."

"I've never seen *Close Encounters.*

"You should. But we're not going to solve this problem talking about it. Let's get busy on Colonel West. Do you just call the Pentagon?"

"Not exactly."

Bill got up and went into his office, sat at his desk, and started looking up phone numbers on his computer. Morgen followed him and was immediately drawn to the hundreds of books crammed into bookshelves on the other side of the room from his desk.

Bill called an old friend who covered military affairs for The Washington Post. They hadn't spoken since Bill left the Times a decade ago but stayed in touch with Christmas cards.

"Max Burris."

"Max, this is a voice out of your past. It's Bill Sanders."

"Bill, for God's sake. I figured you'd never talk to us poor working-press slobs again. How are you? Where are you? Are you in D.C.?"

"No. At Home. In New York."

"I've been seeing stories about this novel you've got coming out in the fall. Looks like you're going to hit the jackpot again."

"Maybe. I hope so. My agent hopes so."

"So, what's up? What can I do for you?

"I need your help tracking down a couple of military guys I used to deal with. I don't want to try to do it myself because I don't have any press credentials anymore. If I called the Pentagon I'd just get shuffled around by clerks. Plus, I don't want it on record that I called the Pentagon. I don't want to get anybody in trouble."

"Whoa, tell you what. Let's meet for coffee and talk about this."

"Well, I guess that's okay. I hadn't planned on coming to Washington anytime soon. But I can. I could take the Acela down tonight. I may bring a research assistant with me."

"No problem. Let's meet at ten at that coffee shop we used to go to. You remember it?"

"Sure. I think it was called ...."

"Great. See you then. Gotta go. Got a call on the other line."

Bill put the phone in its cradle and looked up to a view of Morgen's not unattractive backside. She was bending over to look at some books on a lower shelf. *I've been too isolated the last couple of years writing that novel. I haven't been around enough people, especially unattached women. But I don't know if Morgen's unattached. Maybe I should ask her. What about that roommate? Of course, I could end up spoiling what appears to be a good working relationship so far, even if she is acting a little bossy at times.*

His thoughts snapped back to Max Burris. *Why did he turn secretive when I mentioned a couple of military guys I was looking for? Why didn't he want to talk on the phone? Is his phone tapped? Is mine? If someone was listening, they know I'm going to D.C. this afternoon on the train and could easily track me to the coffee shop tomorrow morning if that's what Max was worried about.* Bill was getting that same queasy feeling he got when he heard Warren Holden had died. *I don't know what kind of a weird game this is, but maybe two can play.*

"Morgen."

She stood up and turned around.

"You sure have some interesting books here."

"Thanks, but we've suddenly got some important things to do. Can you go to Washington with me tonight and attend a short meeting with a Post reporter in the morning?"

"Sure. I couldn't help but overhear your half of the call. I'm yours for at least a month. Remember?"

"Right. Go home and pack for an overnight trip. Then come back here. While you're doing that, I'll make a hotel reservation and book us on the shuttle."

"I've always found the train to be more efficient and certainly more pleasant."

"I agree. But tonight, we fly. When you get back I'll explain why.

After she left, Bill turned to his computer and booked two tickets on the four o'clock American Airlines shuttle. He picked up the phone and reserved two adjoining rooms at the Hay-Adams Hotel. Then he called George and ordered a car and driver to pick them up at two-thirty for a trip to LaGuardia Airport.

On the way to LaGuardia, Bill recounted his odd conversation with Max Burris.

"It was like his phone was tapped and he didn't want

someone to know who I was looking for or where we were meeting. Because I had told him I could take the train, I decided to take the shuttle instead. Maybe he's just being careful and doesn't want to get anyone at the Pentagon in trouble for talking to a reporter. But I got the distinct impression he thought our conversation wasn't private."

"Do people in Washington routinely record phone calls?"

"Not in my day. At least I didn't think so. But it's been more than ten years since I worked there. Remember all that NSA stuff. I guess maybe things have changed. Or been revealed."

The next morning, after some room service coffee, Bill and Morgen walked five blocks to the Sunrise Coffee Shop. They walked in the front door a few minutes before ten; Max Burris waved at them from a table in the back.

Max stood and gave Bill a bear hug before being introduced to Morgen. Ten years had left Max's waist a bit thicker and his black hair more than a little grayer. His dark eyes were as intense as always.

A waiter took their order for coffee and breakfast sandwiches.

"What's the deal, Max? Why were you so secretive on the phone yesterday? You got me so worried that we took the shuttle instead of the train like I said I would. By the way, Morgen is part of whatever we talk about. She knows everything I know."

"Jesus, you've been away from this town too long. The NSA scandal is only the tip of the iceberg. Reporters have to assume their phones are tapped. You call me up and want to discuss by names a couple of sources you had at the Pentagon. You can't talk about stuff like that on the phone. I cut you off because you were about to mention the name of this place. Taking the shuttle was a good move, I guess. I've just had one too many weird experiences where some official seems to know what I'm doing before I do it. And I'm not the only one. The whole town is getting more than a little paranoid."

Max seemed strained and tense, not the easy-going reporter Bill had known a decade ago. He talked faster than Bill remembered.

"Relax, Max. I'm just trying to track down a retired colonel who might not want to be found for a project I'm working on. I thought if those two old sources of mine were still at the Pentagon they might be able to help. But I want to talk to them off the record. And I don't want to stir anything up by inquiring about them. You can do that discreetly without raising any alarms. Hell, you could probably find my retired colonel for me, but you're a busy guy and I've imposed enough already."

"That sounds pretty harmless. Let me see what I can do. What are their names?"

"James Keller and Lawrence Sullivan. They were both Army majors when I knew them." *I must be going soft. I just revealed the names of two important sources from ten years ago to a Washington Post reporter and a woman I hardly know. But I trust Max, and I guess I decided to trust Morgen when I hired her.*

Max pulled a reporter's notebook out of his inside jacket pocket and wrote down the two names.

"Max, you've got to promise me you'll keep this between us. Those guys could get in a world of trouble for talking to me when I was a reporter."

"You know me better than that. I'll even burn this page out of my notebook when I'm finished. I'll call your cell in an hour or two. What's the number?"

Bill slipped a business card out of his wallet and handed it to Max.

"Where are you staying?"

"The Hay-Adams."

Max nodded to Morgen and left without another word.

Bill called the hotel and arranged for a late checkout time.

*

Bill and Morgen walked around Washington for the next hour and a half. Bill explained the importance of her never disclosing the names of Keller or Sullivan to anyone. Morgen assured him she could be trusted with confidential information. She then insisted Bill go over some of the events in Jefferson again in case he might remember some important detail he had missed.

They were in Lafayette Park in front of the White House when Bill's cell rang. Max's name flashed on the screen.

"Hi, Max."

"Here's the deal. The first guy is retired. Lives in some upcountry village in Thailand. The second is now a bird colonel. Still at the Pentagon. Check at your hotel's front desk for an envelope."

No names and no numbers over the phone.

"Thanks, Max. I owe you."

"How about dinner when the royalties start rolling in from that novel?"

"Sure thing. Plan on coming to New York in the fall."

"Sounds good. Gotta go. Burned the notebook page. Bye."

Bill and Morgen walked a few steps to the Hay-Adams and picked up the envelope at the front desk. It contained a single sheet of white paper with a phone number penciled in the center.

Bill dialed the number. He wondered if Larry Sullivan would remember their secret arrangement for meeting.

"Colonel Sullivan."

"Larry, it's Bill Sanders."

"Bill Sanders! Are you in D.C.?"

"Yep. For the day. It would be great to see you again."

The phone went dead as Larry Sullivan hung up.

Morgen gave Bill a puzzled look.

"What now?"

"I'll meet you back at the hotel. I'm going to the zoo."

An hour later, Bill was standing at the entrance to the National Zoo's Elephant Trails exhibit. He came alone because he didn't want Larry to be spooked by a stranger.

"Mr. Bill."

Bill turned and there was Larry, sweaty and in jogging clothes. His red hair had turned a bit blonder; his freckles seemed more prominent. Bill suddenly realized he looked a lot like a shorter version of Paul.

They shook hands and sat together on a nearby bench.

"It's been a long time, Bill."

"I was afraid you would forget our code for meeting here."

"Not a chance. We did it too many times. I always trusted you. I knew you'd go to jail before you'd blow my cover as a source."

"Absolutely."

"So, what's up after all these years?"

"I'm trying to track down a retired colonel named Richard West. There's not much about him in the public record. I can't even find out where he lives. He worked in NATO and at the Pentagon, according to what little I found in the public library. He's seventy-two."

"Why are you looking for him?"

"It's complicated. It's best if I don't explain it now. But I promise I will later."

"Okay. Like I said, I trust you. I've never heard of this guy but let me start poking around. I'll be in touch in a day or so. You said you were in D.C. for the day. Does that mean you're going back to New York tonight?"

"Yes."

"Later, then."

Larry stood up and waved as he jogged away.

Bill met Morgen back at the hotel.

"What was that all about?"

"Let's get checked out. I'll explain everything in the taxi to Union Station."

"Thought we were flying."

"Thought you liked the train."

CHAPTER 24

"Bill, is everything all right?"

"Sure. Are we still on for lunch today?"

"Of course."

"Okay. See you at Dave's at one."

As he put down the phone, Bill realized how curt he had been in talking with Nancy Luke. *The past few weeks are getting to me. Got to calm down.*

Bill had given Morgen the day off after they got back from Washington the night before. He promised to call her the minute he heard anything from Larry Sullivan.

✳

Bill's mood improved after walking to Dave's. It was a clear, warm day. It felt good to be back in New York.

He arrived fifteen minutes early and took a seat at their regular table. Gerald, their usual waiter, sat a glass of water in from of him.

"Welcome, Mr. Sanders. Can I get you a drink or a menu? Or would you rather wait until Ms. Luke arrives?"

"I'll wait, Gerald. Thanks."

"Very good, Sir."

Nancy arrived ten minutes later.

She ordered a glass of Chardonnay. Bill hesitated and then decided on a glass of Cabernet Sauvignon.

"What's wrong, Bill?"

"Nothing. What do you mean?"

"Well, you get back in town and stay in a hotel instead of

your apartment. You don't call me. I have to find out from a gossip that you're home. I know we're not close friends, but I am your agent and you're my most valuable client. We have a strong professional relationship. I just felt like you were avoiding or ignoring me. And when I called this morning about lunch you were more than a little short."

"Nancy, I'm really sorry. I didn't mean to offend you in any way. It's just that my trip to Indiana turned into a nightmare when Paul was killed. And the business with his daughter is complex and confusing. I guess it left me more rattled than I thought."

"The girl is still missing?"

"Yes. For more than a month now. It's a nightmare for her mother and grandparents."

Gerald interrupted to take their orders. Both had the grilled salmon.

"What are you going to do now?"

"It's unclear. I'm working on some leads that I haven't even talked to Paul's wife about. But I think the odds are high that Cindy's dead."

"Will you stay in town?"

"I don't know. Nancy, there's some stuff about this Indiana business that I can't talk about, not even to you. But I promise when it's all over I'll tell you everything. And some of it is very weird. Just trust me for a while."

"Of course."

While they were eating, Bill brought up his idea for a book on the Middle East patterned after *Points South*.

"It's a great idea, but it has to be as strong as *Points South*. Otherwise they'll declare you over the hill. You know what the critics are like."

"I think I can pull it off."

"So do I."

Over coffee, their conversation turned to business. Nancy said a major Hollywood producer had offered half a million dollars for the movie rights to *Look Down*. She wanted to turn it down and hold out for more.

"That's a lot of money, Nancy."

"They really want this movie. They expect us to reject their first offer. It's just a game of numbers to them. When other producers hear we turned down this offer, they may jump in. We could have a bidding war on our hands."

"Well, you're one of the best agents in New York, and you haven't steered me wrong yet. Do it."

"I'll call when they counter. And they will. Soon."

As they were leaving Dave's, Bill gave Nancy a kiss on the cheek and squeezed her hand.

*

When Bill returned to his apartment building, George stopped him in the lobby.

"Some kid left this for you, Mr. Sanders. About an hour ago." He handed Bill a white, letter-size envelope with his name printed on it in child-like block letters.

"Thanks, George."

Bill opened the envelope in the elevator. Inside was a single sheet of white paper with the same block-letter printing: IT WOULD BE GREAT TO SEE YOU AGAIN. NOON TOMORROW. *No phone calls. No text messages. Nothing that can be traced or recorded.*

Once inside his apartment, Bill called Morgen.

"Listen, I've got to go back to D.C. in the morning, but I'll be back sometime in the afternoon. I'll call you the minute I land. Let's have dinner tomorrow night and I'll fill you in on everything."

"You sure you don't want me to go with you?

"Yep. I have to do this by myself. Same reason as before. Another person might spook him."

"That'll be two days off for me. You're a pretty laid-back boss."

"Brace yourself. I have a feeling things may change."

Bill was eating some peanuts when Larry Sullivan jogged up to the entrance of the National Zoo's Elephant Trails exhibit at exactly noon.

"Bill Sanders. What a pleasure seeing you again." Larry motioned toward the nearby bench where they first sat two days ago.

"Want some peanuts?"

"No, thanks. I'll hold out for some cold water."

Bill lowered his voice. "Did you find out anything about West?"

"Jesus H. Christ. You really know how to pick them. You said on Tuesday that you'd explain later what this is all about. To be honest, I don't think I want to know."

"What do you mean?"

"This guy Richard West? The lid is on him. Tight. He is so classified and buried in secrecy that I even raised some eyebrows by asking about him. I explained that a distant cousin of his who knew me was trying to find him. That seemed to satisfy the eyebrows.

"People I know with really high security clearances can't find out anything. The CIA, the NSA and military intelligence operations have blocked all computer access to anything about West. He's basically been disappeared. Hell, you found out more about him in the public library than I did with every source I could pump."

"Why all the secrecy? West must be doing something the government doesn't want us or somebody to know about."

"Or some part of the government. Everything's so compartmentalized these days that very few ever see the big picture. Sometimes I wonder if there even is one."

"West's last assignment before he retired was a five-year stint with NATO in Brussels. I wonder if looking there would turn up anything. Do you have any NATO contacts?"

"One or two, now that you mention it. That might be worth chasing. NATO's a lot looser than the U.S. military, especially when it comes to security. Too many countries with too many competing interests. It can be a hotbed of intrigue and gossip. It's also a posh assignment. I did a six-month tour there two years ago. There's plenty of high-level concern about food and wine. NATO aircraft spend a lot of hours flying wine from Spain and Italy to Brussels."

"Could you set me up with somebody if I went to Brussels?"

"Maybe, but I'll have to think about it. The NATO guys I know haven't been there long enough to know West. If he's seventy-two now, that means he's been retired for almost ten years. What we need is somebody who's been around a while and knew him and maybe knows where he headed when he left Brussels. Let me work on this. You'll hear from me."

"Through your kids' brigade?"

Larry smiled, stood up, and jogged off with a wave of his right hand.

*

"Hello."

"Morgen, it's Bill. I just landed at LaGuardia. Let's have dinner. I made a reservation at Smith and Wollensky for seven. "

"That's the famous steak place?"

"Yep. I'm in the mood for steak if you are."

"Why not?"

"I'll meet you there. I'm going to go to my apartment first for a shower and to get a jacket."

"Where is this place?"

"On Third Avenue at Forty-Ninth Street. Can't miss it."

"Okay. See you at seven."

*

Bill arrived at the restaurant a few minutes early and was immediately seated. He ordered a Grey Goose martini. He hoped his reference to wearing a jacket was enough of a reminder to Morgen that this wasn't a jeans and T-shirt place.

The waiter brought his martini; he had just begun to sip it when Morgen arrived and was escorted to their table. She was wearing a dark-blue pants suit, low-cut heels, and a white blouse. Her hair was loose and tossed back, showcasing ruby earrings that dangled from her pierced ears.

Bill was momentarily taken aback. *She is beautiful. And elegant. I didn't know she had pierced ears. I guess I just didn't notice.*

Morgen was seated and ordered a glass of Merlot.

"How'd it go in D.C.? Did your friend find West?"

"No. Apparently the government doesn't want him to be found. But Larry's working another angle. I'll know more in a day or two, I think. We may have to fly to Brussels for a few days. Can you do that?"

"Sure. I'm yours for a month. Remember? Why Brussels?"

"West's last assignment before he retired was with NATO. Larry's trying to find someone who knew him then and might know where he went when he left Brussels."

"Sounds like a long shot."

"I guess, but it's all we have. And I'm determined to follow every lead. I've got too much invested. If we fail, it won't be because we didn't try."

A waiter came to take their orders. They both selected shrimp cocktails to start. Morgen ordered a medium filet mignon with Roquefort cheese; Bill asked for prime rib, medium rare. Both ordered a side of creamed spinach.

"Have you been to Brussels before?"

"When I worked for the Times I was there on a couple of presidential trips. Then Jane and I were there a couple of times on vacation. You?"

"No. I was in Europe for the summer between my junior and senior years as an undergrad. But never got to Brussels. I hear the beer and food are great."

"Yep, but the Belgians use mayonnaise on their French fries."

The next morning Bill was sipping coffee in his apartment and trying to make sense of jumbled and confusing dreams about Morgen, Brussels, and UFOs. *Probably the result of too much rich food at Smith and Wollensky.*

The door buzzer interrupted his musings. It was George.

"Morning, Mr. Sanders. Some kid left this for you in the lobby."

George handed Bill a white envelope like the previous one. Bill's name was printed on it in the same child-like block letters as the first.

"Was it the same kid who left the envelope on Wednesday?"

"No. That was a boy. This was a girl. Probably ten or eleven, I would guess. She put the envelope on the desk and ran out without talking to anyone. Just like the boy did."

"Thanks, George." Bill handed him a ten-dollar bill.

Bill tore open the envelope. Inside, printed on a piece of white paper, was a name and address:

JEFFREY CONWAY
AVE. DES HANNETONS 1640
WATERMAEL-BOITSFORT
1170 BRUXELLES

There was no phone number. Bill knew Watermael-Boitsfort was an upscale neighborhood, or commune, of Brussels. He went to his computer and Googled a map of the city and found Avenue des Hannetons.

He called Morgen.

"I need your passport number. We're going to Brussels."

"When?" She sounded a bit groggy.

"Tonight. If I can get reservations."

"Well, hold on a minute while I get my passport."

Bill realized he had probably awakened Morgen. He looked at his watch. Eight-thirty.

Morgen returned to the phone and Bill copied her passport number and her full name: Morgen Leslie Remley.

"I need to make our travel arrangements. I'll be back in touch later this morning."

"I'll start packing."

"Me, too."

A few minutes after ten Bill logged onto the Delta Air Lines website and booked two one-way business-class tickets on a flight that would leave JFK at seven-thirty that evening and arrive in Brussels at nine-fifteen Saturday morning. *Since I don't know exactly when we're coming back, best not to buy round-trip tickets. If we have to wait a day or two to get return seats at least we won't starve.*

Then he searched for hotels and selected the Hilton in central Brussels. He booked adjoining rooms for an early arrival Saturday.

Finally, to the Hertz website where he arranged for a Volvo to be waiting for them at Zaventem Airport.

He dialed Morgen's number again.

"I'm not packed yet."

"Neither am I. But we have reservations. We leave from JFK at seven-thirty. How about if I get a car and driver and pick you up at your place at two? That should put us at JFK by three or three-thirty at the latest. That'll give us plenty of time."

"Sounds good."

Morgen gave Bill her address on Summit Street in Carroll Gardens.

Bill's driver pulled in front of the three-story brownstone at five minutes past two. Bill got out of the car, walked up the front steps and rang the bell for the first floor. The name plaque above the bell read Remley/Jones.

The main door buzzed open and Bill entered a hallway leading to stairs on the right and a door to the first-floor apartment on the left. It opened and there was Morgen, wearing a tan pants suit and blue sneakers.

"All set?"

Yes. Let me just get my suitcase. Oh, come in and meet my roommate."

Bill stepped past Morgen into the apartment and was met by an older woman who appeared to be in her late sixties.

"Brenda Jones, this is Bill Sanders. The writer I was telling you about."

"Nice to meet you, Mr. Sanders. Morgen is a big fan of yours."

"Good to meet you, too, Brenda. Sorry we have to rush off, but we have a plane to catch and our car is waiting."

"I understand. Off you go. See you when you get back, Morgen. Hope to see you again, Mr. Sanders."

On the way to the airport, Bill couldn't resist asking about Brenda Jones.

"How did you wind up with a roommate twice your age."

"She's the aunt of a friend of mine from Kansas. Her husband died last year in Topeka, where he was a cardiologist. They had no children. After his death, she decided to move to New York. It was apparently something she had always wanted to do. I think her niece was shocked, but she called me for help. She said her aunt needed someplace to live until she could get herself organized and be comfortable living on her own. I needed help with the rent, so I agreed to convert a small den into a second bedroom. We've become great friends. She loves New York, especially the theater. I think she's seen every play on and off Broadway. I dread the day she decides to move out and be on her own."

"I can understand that. She seems very nice." *Mystery of the roommate solved.*

CHAPTER 25

It was raining steadily when the Delta jet touched down at the Brussels airport. It was still raining when Bill pulled the rental Volvo in front of the Hilton Hotel. A bellman took his and Morgen's luggage out of the trunk; a valet slipped behind the wheel to park the car.

Once settled in their rooms, they decided to rest a bit and hope the rain would end before heading out to look for Jeffrey Conway.

Bill took a shower, put on the hotel's terrycloth bathrobe, and stretched out on the king-size bed. He had just begun to doze when he was roused by a knock at the door.

"Who is it?"

"Morgen."

"Just a minute."

Bill quickly ran a comb through his hair before opening the door. Morgen was standing there, barefoot, in a similar hotel robe. Her hair was still wet from showering.

"Can we talk?"

"Sure. Come on in. What's up?"

"This is awkward for me, but this adjoining room business is getting a little old. Not to mention expensive for you."

"I can afford it."

"I know you can. But Bill, we're adults. Normal people. Both single. What I'm trying to say is I'm attracted to you, and I wonder how you feel about that."

"Morgen, I've been attracted to you since you first introduced yourself to me in the library. Your perfume ... you were so beautiful at dinner Thursday night. You have no idea how relieved I was to find out your roommate wasn't a twenty-something hunk. But I'm basically nervous about these things. I figured our age difference was a barrier. I'm twenty years older than you. And, to be honest, I'm still getting over my wife's death after two years. I made one try at a relationship with a teacher in New Jersey. That was a disaster, and the fault was all mine. I'm out of practice and clumsy at these things. But that's all history. To answer your question, I feel great that you're attracted to me. And, yes, the feeling is mutual. Come here."

Bill pulled Morgen toward him as she opened her robe and let it fall to the floor.

By the time they reached the bed, Bill's robe was also on the floor.

By early afternoon, the rain had stopped; the city glistened in the afternoon sunlight.

Bill and Morgen decided to postpone their search for Conway until Sunday. They showered again, dressed and went down to the lobby where they picked up a map of Brussels from the concierge. They spent almost two hours in the Royal Museum of Fine Arts. Morgen was fascinated by the Magritte collection. Bill was fascinated by Morgen.

After the museum, they took a long walk around the center of the city, ending up at the Grand Place. Bill remembered the Restaurant 'T Kelderke from previous trips. The vaulted dining room was as warm and welcoming as always. Before looking at the menu, they each had a bottle of Orval ale made by Trappist monks in the south of Belgium.

"So, you've been here before. What do you recommend?"

"You can never go wrong in Belgium with moules and frites. Mussels and French fries. The steamed mussels are served in whatever kind of sauce you like. I think it's the national dish of Belgium."

"Sounds delicious. What are you having?"

"Waterzooi."

"What's that?"

"A kind of chicken stew with vegetables in a cream sauce. It's Flemish. Very good."

A waiter wearing a long white apron approached their table.

Morgen ordered the moules in a white wine sauce; Bill, the waterzooi.

Before the waiter turned to go to the kitchen, Morgen raised her hand.

"Madame?"

"I'll have some mayonnaise with my frites, please."

"Oui, Madame."

*

After dinner, they decided to walk back to the hotel. It was a warm evening and there were still streaks of pale light in the sky.

"Why did the waiter call me 'madame'?"

"I guess he was just being polite. My French is pretty poor, but I think it's a polite form of address for a woman when her marital status isn't known."

"Oh."

*

Bill and Morgen slept in Sunday morning and ordered breakfast from room service.

"Bill, do you think Sunday morning is a good time to go looking for Jeffrey Conway?"

"Maybe. Aren't people usually home on Sunday?"

"Unless they're at church."

"By the time we get going, church should be over."

"True. Do we know anything about Conway?"

"Nothing. Before we left New York, I Googled him. There were lots of Jeffrey Conways but I couldn't figure out if one of them was our guy or not. None of them lived in Brussels, but that may not mean anything."

It was after noon by the time they finished breakfast, got dressed and called for the car. The concierge used a red marker to show them the route to Avenue des Hannetons on a map.

As they were driving away from the hotel, Bill turned to Morgen.

"If we find this guy, let's agree to give him as little information as possible. This whole thing is much too weird to get into with a stranger. All he needs to know is that we're looking for West because he may be able to help us find someone else."

"I agree. Why don't you do most of the talking? Just introduce me as your assistant."

Twenty minutes later they parked on the street in front of a three-story brick town house, No. 1640, the end unit of the row. The front yard and the entire street were lined with ornamental cherry trees in full bloom, giving the whole street a pink hue. They walked toward the house and followed a concrete walkway that led to a side door with a buzzer and an intercom.

Bill looked at Morgen. She nodded and he pressed the buzzer.

Nothing. No sounds from within. No lights.

Bill knocked on the metal-framed glass door.

Suddenly, the intercom crackled to life.

"Yes. Can I help you?"

"Mr. Conway?"

"Yes."

"My name is Bill Sanders. I'm a writer from New York. Morgen Remley, my assistant, is with me. I wonder if we could talk with you for a few minutes."

"Are you a reporter?"

"No. I used to be. Now I write books."

"What do you want to talk about?"

"We're trying to find somebody, and we think you may be able to help us."

"Hold on."

In a few seconds the door swung open.

Jeffrey Conway stepped back and invited Bill and Morgen in.

"Let's go upstairs," he said, motioning them to follow him up a staircase to the left that led to a living room, dining room, and kitchen on the second floor. The furniture was Danish modern. A tri-colored cat was stretched out on a sofa next to a small brick fireplace.

Conway was a short, rotund man with white hair and a white beard. His round, horn-rimmed glasses had thick lenses and gave him an owlish look that was emphasized by a nervous blink. A stethoscope hung from his neck.

"Oh, sorry about that." He removed the stethoscope and put it on the dining room table next to a blood pressure cuff. "I was just taking my blood pressure when you buzzed. Please have a seat."

He directed them to two chairs in front of the sofa.

"Can I get you anything?"

"Just some water, please," Morgen replied.

"Mr. Sanders?"

"Water would be fine. Thanks."

Conway went into the kitchen and returned with a bottle of Spa water and three glasses. He sat on the sofa next to the cat.

"What's this all about? Who are you looking for?" He blinked at Bill.

"A retired colonel named Richard West. He spent the last five years of his career assigned to NATO and we understand you were friends with him."

"Why are you looking for him?"

"I've been trying to help a friend find a missing person and some people I've talked to think West might be able to help. But we can't find him." Bill didn't mention that the missing person was a ten-year-old girl or that his friend, the girl's father, was dead. Nothing about the other deaths or UFOs. *Keep it simple so he won't get suspicious.*

Morgen looked at Bill and give him an almost imperceptible nod, a reinforcement of the decision they made in the car a few minutes earlier.

Conway seemed to accept Bill's explanation. He blinked a few times, took a sip of water, and smiled.

"You said you write books. Did you write that book on South America that everybody was raving about?"

"Yes. I confess."

Well, I'm not much of a reader. But a lot of my friends said it was a good book."

"Thanks."

After a lull in the conversation, Conway reached out to pet the sleeping cat and then blinked at both Bill and Morgen.

"I knew Richard West during the last three years he was here. Inasmuch as anyone could know him. He was a very secretive man. He kept to himself a lot. But we had a love of chess in common and over time and many matches we became what you might call friends."

"Why were you here, if I may ask?"

"I'm a doctor. I had a private practice in Michigan for fifteen years and grew to hate dealing with insurance companies, filling out more and more forms, and paying outrageous premiums for malpractice insurance. Also, my wife died suddenly of a heart attack. She had been my office nurse. With her gone, I lost interest in the practice. I was just going through the motions. So, when I heard the Air Force was recruiting doctors, I closed my practice and joined. They don't put experienced doctors who join through all the same crap that recruits face. Basically, they made me an officer and put me to work. Not long after, I was transferred here. I retired four years ago and decided to say in Brussels. I like it here. And I don't have much family in the states anymore. I've only been back once in four years. Couldn't wait to get back to Brussels. It's home to me."

"So how did you meet West?"

"As a patient. He came to my clinic with a cold. For some reason I can't remember we got to talking about chess. Then we started playing. Two or three times a month we would have dinner together. He had never been married. He was a very smart guy, but he sure played everything close to the chest."

"He retired nearly ten years ago. Do you know where he went or where he is now?"

"He used to talk about retiring out west somewhere. I only got one letter from him after he left Brussels. But it wasn't from out west. Hold on a minute."

Conway got up carefully so as not to disturb the cat and went upstairs to the third floor. Bill and Morgen could hear him rummaging around in some papers.

He came back downstairs holding a letter. He handed it to Bill.

"The return address is a post office box in Pine Bush, New York. Wherever that is. But that was nine years ago."

The mention of Pine Bush caused the back of Bill's neck to feel tingly. He glanced at Morgen. Her cheeks were flushed.

"You're welcome to read the letter. There's nothing personal or important in it."

Conway was right. The one-page letter, in very precise cursive, thanked Conway for all the good chess games and dinners together. It also thanked him for the good medical care West had received. No mention of exactly where he was living, what he was doing, or his plans for the future. It was signed, "Best, Richard."

"You haven't heard from him since this letter."

"Not a word. I wrote back but never got a reply."

That tingly feeling stuck with Bill as they drove away from Dr. Conway's house.

"Pine Bush! West could be in Pine Bush. Jesus, Morgen, that's one of the seven UFO cases you gave me to research. That could link Colonel West to UFOs and explain why Warren Holden sent me his name."

"Does this mean we're headed back to New York?"

"Yes, but let's slow down a little. Let's think this through and enjoy each other's company for a couple of days. You've never been to Bruges. I guarantee you'll love it. Let's check out of the Hilton, drive to Bruges and spend a couple of nights there. We can try to get reservations to fly back Wednesday. What do you think?"

"Adjoining rooms?"

"Not a chance."

CHAPTER 26

"So now what?"

Morgen, wearing a pair of silk pajamas and sitting in the club chair in Bill's living room, which was bathed in sunlight from the east-facing windows, paused to take another sip of coffee from a white mug. She and Bill had arrived Wednesday evening from Brussels. They spent the night in his apartment.

"I'm not sure. Rushing off to Pine Bush to look for a secretive man who had a post office box there nine years ago sounds like a wild goose chase to me. I think we ultimately may need to go there, because it's the only real clue we have. But I also want to give the whole thing more thought. Are we missing something? Also, before we do anything else I want to call the Sheriff in Jefferson as well as Sharon to see if there have been any new developments."

"Okay. Why don't I go home and get myself unpacked and organized while you make those calls? I'll be back early in the afternoon and you can fill me in."

As Morgen was changing into jeans and a T-shirt, Bill rummaged around in his desk and found a spare apartment key. He walked into the bedroom and handed it to her.

"Just in case. You may need to get in here sometime when I'm not home."

"True. Thanks."

Bill nodded as he reached for the phone to call George and arrange a car and driver for Morgen.

"Dave, it's Bill Sanders. Just wanted to check in with you."

"Well, there's not much to report here. The state police got the FBI involved in investigating Cindy Watson's disappearance. A couple of agents have camped out here, but I'm not sure how much help they'll be. We finally released Daniel Scott's body to his parents. They actually came here from Denver to sign the paperwork, which they didn't have to do. I think they really just wanted to see where Daniel lived and worked. Nice people. Neal had them over to his house for dinner. They asked a lot of questions about the case but never really pressured me about solving it. They just asked me to call and keep them informed."

"Have you talked to Sharon?"

"Yeah, a couple of times. She seems to be holding things together pretty well. She calls about Cindy, but there's nothing new I can tell her."

"Well, I don't know anything new either. But let's stay in touch. If I don't hear from you, I'll call back in a week or so."

"Okay. Take care."

"Bye."

Before calling Sharon, Bill opened the top drawer of his desk and pulled out the map of Madison County he took from Daniel Scott's room and the note he found in his duffel after the break-in at Paul's. He studied the map with its random pattern of Os and Xs. He knew he was concealing evidence, but evidence of what? *O equals UFO sightings. X equals helicopters. Maybe I should just fly out to Indiana and come clean with Dave. But not yet. Maybe soon, but not yet.*

"Sharon?"

"Yes."

"It's Bill Sanders."

"Bill, it's good to hear from you. How's the rewrite on the novel going?" *She sounds too cheerful.*

"Fine. I just wanted to check in and see how you're doing and find out if there's anything new or anything I can do."

"Nothing on both counts. Paul's still dead and Cindy's still missing."

Sharon started to sob.

"Oh, Bill, what am I going to do? I can't stand this much longer. At least I know what happened to Paul. I can't stand not knowing about Cindy. Is she dead? Kidnapped? Some of my friends have stopped calling. They don't know what to say, I guess. A few think Paul had something to do with Cindy's disappearance, despite evidence to the contrary. And then I find out about you!"

"Me?"

"Yes, you. I was going through some papers in Paul's desk and found a notebook in which he had written snippets of conversations he had with you. He told you his story about Cindy being abducted by a UFO. He also told you that he told Dave Taylor and me. He was obviously having a psychotic breakdown. That may have been the reason he crashed his Jeep."

Sharon was screaming now.

"Why didn't you talk to me? We might have saved him!"

"Sharon, you weren't there. You had left to go to your parents in Indianapolis. I thought he might be telling ...."

"You could have called me, you bastard! You didn't do anything about this UFO fantasy he concocted, and now he's dead. I hate you! I never want to talk to you or see you again!"

Bill held the phone in his hand for a few seconds after Sharon hung up. He was stunned. *This is what I get for being secretive. I should have put everything out in the open with Sharon and Dave. Or never gotten involved in the first place. I'm a writer, not a goddamn detective or psychologist.*

He put the phone back in its cradle and when into the kitchen to get another cup of coffee.

The phone rang. *Probably Sharon calling to apologize.*

"Hello."

"I'm unpacked. I'll be there in about an hour if that's okay."

"That's great. See you then." *This may be the end of our adventure. Hope it's not the end of us.*

Bill headed back to the kitchen when the phone rang again.

"Hello."

"Bill Sanders?"

"Yes."

"I understand you've been looking for me. This is Richard West."

CHAPTER 27

"Why the worried look?"

Morgen let herself into the apartment to find Bill staring out the south window at the United Nations building.

"You're never going to believe who called right after you did."

"Who?"

"Colonel Richard West."

"What? From where? What did he say?"

"I don't know where he was calling from. His number showed up as 'unknown caller' on my phone. He said he understood I was looking for him. He wouldn't answer any questions on the phone. Said he wanted to meet with us."

"But how can we meet him if we don't know where he is?"

"This is where it gets a little strange."

"How?"

"He wants to meet us, but only on his terms. He said a car would pick us up in front of the apartment at six."

"Six today?"

"Yes. He said we would then be driven for about two hours to wherever he is. He also said he would only meet us if we agreed to be blindfolded during the two-hour drive. He also said we had to agree not to say one word to each other during the trip."

"Did you agree to that?"

"Yes. I didn't know what else to do. Not if we want to get to the bottom of this mess."

"I guess. But this gives me the creeps. How do we know this guy isn't some kind of psycho?"

"I guess we don't. I've been thinking. Maybe you shouldn't go. Maybe I should go alone."

"No, I signed on for at least a month. You were straight with me and told me everything. I'm going. End of discussion."

"I guess you're right. He knew your name and specifically talked about meeting with the two of us."

"What do we do between now and six?"

"Let's get some Chinese food delivered. I haven't had any lunch."

"Me neither."

"No use traveling hungry."

At a quarter of six, Bill and Morgen took the elevator to the lobby and walked out onto the sidewalk in front of Eastside Towers. Cross-town traffic was heavy on Seventy-Second Street but was beginning to ease a bit from the rush-hour peak.

At exactly six, a black Chevrolet Suburban SUV with U.S. government license plates pulled in front of the apartment. *A government car?* The side windows were darkened so it was impossible to see inside. Bill had a sudden flashback to Josh Baker's description of the helicopter he said he saw flying around just before Paul's fatal crash: *It was all black and didn't have no markings. And the windows was all dark. Like them limousines you see on TV.*

The passenger door opened and a tall, muscular man in a black suit stepped out onto the sidewalk. A second similar looking man in a dark blue suit stayed in the driver's seat.

"Bill Sanders? Morgen Remley?"

Both nodded.

"Get in, please." The man reached out to open the SUV's rear door, making no effort to conceal a holstered Glock pistol that was clipped to his belt. *What the hell am I getting into? Or getting Morgen into?*

When Bill and Morgen were settled in the rear seat, Black Suit closed the rear door and slid into the passenger seat. After he had closed his door, he twisted around to face Bill and Morgen.

"I think you understand the terms." He handed them both black, heavy velvet hoods. "Put these over your heads and don't remove them until we tell you to. Understand? Also, no talking whatsoever until you're told it's okay to do so. Do you understand that also?"

They nodded again and pulled the hoods over their heads.

As the SUV pulled away from the curb, Morgen slipped her hand into Bill's and squeezed it.

For a while Bill tried to track where they were going. But the driver made a series of disorientating turns that left Bill totally confused. After about 15 minutes he gave up and settled back for the ride, still holding Morgen's hand. About a half hour later he thought the road and traffic noise indicated they were on a bridge, but he couldn't be sure because the thick hood muffled sounds. Occasionally Black Suit and Blue Suit would say something to each other, usually about the traffic or which lane was best. They had almost identical voices and speech patterns.

An hour later they were clearly somewhere less urban. Fewer stops and turns. Twenty minutes later they turned right onto a winding road that forced the driver to slow down. In about ten minutes they turned left onto a rutted gravel road. Morgen had relaxed her hand in Bill's but suddenly tightened her grip again as the SUV bounced over the ruts in the road. In a couple of minutes the tires crunched against gravel as they skidded to a stop.

Black Suit turned around and faced Bill and Morgen, still hooded.

"We're here. We will help you out of the car. Keep your hoods on until we tell you to remove them. Do not talk until you are told it is okay to do so. Nod if you understand and agree."

Both nodded for the third time that evening.

Black Suit and the driver got out of the SUV. The driver then opened Morgen's door, held her by the arm, and helped her out of the SUV. Black Suit went through the same routine with Bill.

"All right, walk with us carefully now. We're going to take about ten steps and then come to a set of four steps you will climb. Then we will go through a door. Don't worry, we'll guide you and be with you every step of the way."

Bill could smell wood smoke. At the top of the four stairs they were on some kind of a platform that he suspected was a porch. They were led through a door after being warned to step carefully over the sill. Once through the door, Bill could feel the warmth coming from what was apparently a fireplace to his right. He could barely hear the crackling sounds of flames licking wood. *It's not really cold, but that feels good.* The floor felt like hardwood under his shoes.

"Turn left." Bill wasn't sure if that order came from Black Suit or Blue Suit.

Five more steps and a hand on Bill's chest stopped him.

A few seconds later he heard the unmistakable sound of an elevator door swishing open.

"Straight ahead now. Watch your step."

As Bill stepped into the elevator, he wondered where Morgen was. Then he smelled her musky perfume and knew she had been led into the elevator ahead of him.

The door hissed shut and the elevator started to descend.

After a few seconds, the elevator thumped to a stop and Bill heard the doors open. Black Suit or Blue Suit gently pushed him through the doors. The air was cooler, and Bill felt padded carpet under his shoes.

"Turn left, please."

As Bill turned, he did not hear a similar command for Morgen. He couldn't smell her perfume outside the elevator. He had no sense of where she was.

After about twenty steps, Bill was told to stop. He heard a door open on his right.

"Turn right. I'm going to lead you through a door into a room."

Once inside, Bill was guided to a chair and told to sit down. The chair had a wooden straight back and a padded seat. His guide then walked back to the door and closed it. Bill heard a deadbolt click into place.

"Okay Mr. Sanders. You may remove the hood and speak if you wish."

Bill pulled the hood off his head. He blinked as his eyes grew accustomed to the harsh overhead florescent lights. He glanced toward the door where Black Suit was standing with his arms crossed in front of his chest. Bill looked around the room. He was seated on a chair next to a wooden desk with a high-backed leather chair. There was a wingback chair and a sofa in front of the desk. There was a small coffee table between the chair and sofa. A lamp and a laptop computer were on the desk, along with a silver tray containing two bottles of Evian water and a glass. Behind the desk was a small kitchen area with a microwave oven. Next to the kitchen was a partially open door leading to a bathroom. The locked door and Black Suit were in front of Bill and slightly to his left. Farther to the left, the side of the room was lined with book-filled shelves and file cabinets. The floor was covered with a thick, slate-colored wall-to-wall carpet.

"Mind if I have a drink of water?"

"Help yourself. That's what it's there for."

Bill put the hood on the desk. He filled the glass half full of water and drained it. He wiped his mouth with the back of his hand and looked at Black Suit.

"Where's Morgen?"

"I can't answer any questions. You'll have to ask the Colonel."

"When will I see him? Can you answer that?"

"I believe in a few minutes. In the meantime, I have to search you and ask that you give me your wallet, cell phone, watch, belt, and anything else you have in your pockets."

Black Suit took the hood from the desk and held it upside down so that it became a velvet bag. Bill stood up and did as he was told. He had to roll his belt up for it to fit into the hood.

Black suit put the hood on the desk and then patted Bill down like any police officer would a suspect. Apparently satisfied, Black Suit scooped up the velvet hood, took a key out of his pocket, and walked to the door. As he unlocked the deadbolt, he turned his head to look at Bill, who had sat back down in the chair.

"Try to relax."

He opened the door and left without saying another word or waiting for a response. The door shut and Bill head the deadbolt click. He was locked in the room alone.

*

Ten minutes went by. Bill drank another half glass of water. He went into the bathroom, relieved himself, and splashed cold water on his face and neck. He dried with a soft white towel hanging next to the sink.

Back in the office, he eased into the leather desk chair. He tried to open the desk drawers; all were locked.

He leaned back in the chair. *This is crazy. What have I gotten into? Locked in an underground room somewhere. Where the hell is Morgen? Why have we been separated?*

A knock on the door interrupted his thoughts.

"Come in. Why are you knocking? Hell, it's your room. Your game."

The deadbolt clicked and the door swung open.

"No need to be testy, Mr. Sanders."

The speaker, leaning heavily on a cane, was a short man with graying hair, sharp features, and flinty green eyes. He wore a dark brown, three-piece suit with a green tie.

He approached Bill and stuck out his right hand. Bill noticed a slight tremor as the hand hung in the air. Someone pulled the door shut from the outside and locked it.

"I'm Richard West. It's a pleasure to meet you at last."

Bill stood and shook the outstretched hand.

"So why am I being held prisoner in this room? Where's my wallet and stuff? What's happened to Morgen? What the hell is going on? Why were we brought here in a government car? Are you working for the government?"

"So many questions. Be patient, Mr. Sanders. All your questions will be answered in good time. Please call me Richard. May I call you Bill?"

"You can call me whatever you like. I just want to know what's going on."

"And you shall. But we have to do this my way. One step at a time. After all, in a way you're the intruder here. You have pried into things you should have left alone. All with good intentions, I realize. You were trying to help a friend find his missing daughter and got in over your head. I was flattered that you flew to Brussels to look for me. But you forgot Will Rogers' advice. You were in a hole and kept digging."

Colonel West suddenly grew pale and winced in pain.

"Sorry, but I'm not well. I have pancreatic cancer and my days are numbered."

"I'm sorry."

"Thanks, but don't be sorry. We all have to die. It's just a matter of when and how. I've come to terms with my death. My only regret is the unanswered questions I'll die with. But for now, let's deal with your questions. Do you mind if we sit in more comfortable accommodations?"

Colonel West walked slowly over to the sofa and eased himself into its soft cushions. He propped his cane within easy reach against the sofa and motioned for Bill to sit in the wingback chair.

"Are you hungry? I expect we'll be here for a while. Maybe all night."

"No. I'm good. Maybe later."

"So, let's talk. We'll take a break in a couple of hours, and I'll order some sandwiches and beer."

A stretch of silence followed. Colonel West loosened his tie and unbuttoned the top button of his dress shirt. Bill sat upright in the wingback chair, wondering what to say or do next.

Colonel West looked directly at Bill. His eyes seemed to

soften a bit.

"What do you know about UFOs—unidentified flying objects?"

"Almost nothing until recently. Then Morgen gave me a crash course."

"Why?"

"Don't ask me questions you know the answers to. I assume you know everything that happened since I went to Indiana to help Paul Watson."

"Don't assume what I know, Bill. Let me repeat: we have to do this my way. I want you to start at the beginning. I want you to tell me in exact detail and in your own words everything you have done and everything that has happened to you since you became involved in this unfortunate girl's disappearance. After that, I shall tell you some things that may clear up matters for you. Or, at least, help you understand the series of events in which you have chosen to become involved. I asked you about UFOs because it seems you gave some credence to what your friend Paul said he saw the night his daughter disappeared."

"Maybe. How do you know? Who have you talked to? What's your involvement in this? Where is Morgen? Is she safe? Is she being held in a locked room too?"

"She's perfectly safe. Please be patient."

"Is our conversation being recorded?"

"Heavens, no! You've been reading too many spy novels. Or, perhaps since your next book is fiction, you have developed an overactive imagination. We're just two men having a conversation, the contents of which must and will be kept secret. No recording. No notes. It's hard to keep something secret if it's recorded. A lesson Richard Nixon learned the hard way."

"What if I don't agree to keep secrets?"

"You will, trust me. But all in good time. Now, start at the beginning. Tell me everything that has happened since you got the call for help from Paul Watson."

CHAPTER 28

Bill relaxed a bit. *What the hell? If replaying events of the past few weeks can lead to some answers, why not? That assumes this guy knows something. If he doesn't, what are we doing here? Secret? We'll see. Also, going through the details of this again might help me see something I missed.*

"Okay, we'll do this your way, Colonel West ... Richard. But in the end, I'd better know a lot more than I know now."

"You will."

Bill adjusted himself more comfortably in the wingback chair and, starting with Paul's first call for help, began at the beginning.

He held back nothing back except details that might identify his sources in D.C. He told Colonel West about the threatening note he found in his luggage at Paul's house and the map he took from Daniel Scott's hotel room. He even explained how the key to Daniel's room showed up in the Wayne Hotel's mail. *I should have come clean about the note, the map, and the key with Dave Taylor a long time ago. I will, when I get out of here.*

Colonel West listened intently as Bill methodically recounted the events that led to him being locked in an underground room somewhere within a two-hour drive from New York City: Bill's drive west to Jefferson; Paul's claim that he saw Cindy in a blue beam of light between a giant UFO and the window to her room; news reports of UFOs around Jefferson; the break-in at Paul's house; Daniel Scott's murder; the security guard's account of strange lights around his house late at night; Paul's drinking problem and his death in a car crash; reports of mysterious helicopters, including the farmer who said he saw a black one flying above Paul's Jeep just before it crashed; the truck fires on the I-65 bridge that caused Bill to miss a flight to Atlanta to talk with Walter Jansen at the Carter Center; the death of Warren Holden; Bill's rush back to New York and his hiding out at the Algonquin Hotel; the message from Holden containing Colonel West's name; meeting Morgen at the library and subsequently hiring her as his research assistant; looking for Colonel West in Brussels only to discover that he apparently disappeared in upstate New York a decade ago; the call from West that brought them here, wherever here is. Upstate New York? New Jersey? Connecticut?

*

Bill finished. West said nothing.

Bill started to look at his wristwatch to see what time it was and then remember it had been taken from him earlier by Black Suit.

"What time is it?"

Colonel West pulled an old-fashioned pocket watch from a slit in his vest.

"Almost midnight. You've been talking nearly two hours. You're a good storyteller. No wonder your books sell so well. I look forward to reading your novel. Ready for some food?"

"Sure."

Colonel West pulled some sort of electronic paging device from another vest pocked and pushed a red button on its top.

"While we wait for the food, answer a question for me, Bill."

"Depends on the question."

"It's another one about UFOs. What do you think is really going on?"

"Well, I'm more convinced of their reality than before I went to Indiana. I covered a so-called UFO sighting early on, as most rookie reporters do. It turned out to be nothing. Until I talked to Paul, I assumed they were hoaxes or products of kooks with overexcited imaginations. I hardly thought about them and knew even less."

"But your recent experiences changed your mind?"

"I think so, to some degree. I think Paul saw something unexplained. I think the security guard was telling the truth. I'm not sure the sightings around Jefferson, a few of which were in the local paper, were hoaxes."

"What do you think is the government's role in all this?"

"Based on what happened in Jefferson and the cases Morgen gave me to study, I would say the government knows more than it admits and works very hard to cover up what it knows. UFO groups are always screaming about a government cover-up. Looks like they have a point. Some even claim the government is in cahoots with the aliens to get access to some of their technology. Others say NASA has secret photographs of UFOs and alien bases on the moon and Mars."

Colonel West smiled.

They were interrupted by a knock on the door.

"Come in," Colonel West said in a loud voice. He did not get up.

The lock clicked and a white-coated waiter pushing a tablecloth-covered cart entered the room. The cart hosted a tray of sandwiches, a basket of potato chips, and an ice bucket containing four bottles of Heineken beer.

The waiter nodded at Colonel West. He then turned and left the room, locking the door behind him.

"Help yourself. There should be ham and roast beef."

The two men ate in silence. When they were finished, Colonel West stood up, without his cane, and pushed the cart to the other side of the room.

He settled back on the sofa.

"Well, I guess it's my turn. But first I own you an apology. I am sorry my men took your watch and other things. That was unnecessary, but a lot of people here have the mentality of policemen, which some of them once were. I have to tolerate at least some of that so that things run smoothly. I hope you understand. You will get your possessions back when we're finished."

"What about the hoods and the secrecy about where we are?"

"I'm afraid that's absolutely necessary, as you will soon understand."

"And Morgen?"

"Her, too, you will soon understand."

CHAPTER 29

Colonel West stood up, this time with the help of his cane, excused himself and went into the bathroom, closing the door tightly behind him. Bill detected a slight limp he hadn't noticed before.

Bill took a sip of water and wondered about Colonel West's comment about Morgen. *Her, too, you will soon understand. What the hell did that mean? Understand what?*

Colonel West came out of the bathroom, his face pale and still a little wet from cold water he had splashed on it. He leaned heavily on his cane as he made his way to the sofa, a sideways limp now clearly evident.

Colonel West settled into the sofa.

"Well, Bill, it's your turn to listen. I just took a couple of pain pills that should carry me through the rest of the night. Brace yourself. Because I'm going to tell you some things that are so secret they aren't even known by most presidents and heads of state. I could be killed for what I'm about to tell you. But I'm dying anyway. So, they'd have to act fast. Plus, killing me would save a lot of pain and suffering on my part. But I'm not concerned about that because you will keep our conversation secret."

"How can you be so sure? I'm a reporter at heart. I love to spill secrets, especially other people's."

"Don't be so sure until we work through this. Remember I said we had to do this my way? I predict that in the end you will find it in your best interest to keep what you have learned to yourself."

"I'm not making any promises, but let's get on with it. Your game, your move."

*

"What I'm going to tell you I will try to make as clear as possible. But thanks to pain medication I may slip up here and there. And things won't always be in chronological order. So, don't hesitate to interrupt me with questions."

"I'm not shy."

"Good."

"First, let's get some unpleasant things out of the way. Your suspicions are correct. I do work for the government. But not in any conventional way, as you shall learn. I work for a small, ultra-secret organization with unlimited funds and virtually unlimited power. Not all the people involved, especially in the field, are always as disciplined as they should be. That can sometimes lead to unintended, and unfortunate, consequences of the kind you saw in Jefferson, Indiana."

"You sound like a lawyer trying to avoid saying something."

"Good point. I'm sorry. Let me be direct. Cindy Watson is dead. My organization is partly responsible for that. I'll give you the details later."

Cindy is dead. He killed her. Just like that. A simple matter of fact. Details to come. Is this prick human? Was he going to let Sharon wonder until the end of her days about what happened to her daughter?

"Things happened very fast after her death. Before I could step in and get control of the situation, some of our field agents panicked, mainly because of your poking around, and killed Daniel Scott. It might have ended there if you hadn't insisted on a paraffin test. These same agents then killed Paul Watson by forcing his car off the road with a helicopter, as you suspected. They were helped by the fact that your friend was drunk. They had concluded he had seen too much and would cause too much trouble. You were next, but the agents knew you had a high profile; they had enough sense to try to scare you away first. They tried to warn you off with the note they left mentioning your late wife, for which I apologize. That was when they trashed your friend's house in an awkward attempt to cover up the removal of a listening device they had earlier attached to the phone line. They also smashed your flip phone, hoping that would force you to get a smart phone that would make it easier to trace your movements. You didn't exactly cooperate when you took so long to replace your smashed phone, but at least you did replace it with a smart one. They staged the truck fires on the bridge in Louisville.

"Before you headed back to New York, I stepped in and put a stop to the carnage. You were hours away from 'committing suicide.' By the way, your friend Warren Holden actually did die of a heart attack. We had nothing to do with his death. Although he was secretly investigating us and threatening to go public, so I'm not sorry he's out of the picture. When he sent you my name the day before he died, I concluded it was time we talked. But I wanted it to be your idea.

Bill felt the blood drain from his face; his chest felt hollow. He took a deep breath.

"What the hell is this government outfit you work for? Murder Inc.? I've got a lot of questions, starting with Cindy and whatever Paul saw the night she disappeared."

"Paul Watson saw what he thought he saw: a UFO. I will answer all your questions, but first let me give you some background information that may change the nature of your questions or eliminate some altogether."

Bill took a drink of water.

"Go on."

"The series of events you have gotten yourself involved in started in Roswell, New Mexico, and the crash of a UFO there in 1947. I believe this was one of the cases Morgen suggested you study. I say this is the start of your story. In fact, there have been sightings of UFOs and contact with aliens for millennia.

There are obvious references to them in the Bible and in ancient texts and mythology. They show up in petroglyphs and painting, some by the masters. The reason it seems like there are more sightings now is that we have a mass media to spread the word."

"Are you saying some kind of a spacecraft really did crash in Roswell? Alien bodies were recovered?"

"Of course. And the Army did a crappy job of covering it up. They even issued a press release saying a flying disk had been recovered. That was quickly retracted, of course, followed by a series of explanations over the years that only the most gullible, which is a majority of the public and the media, believed."

"What happened to the recovered bodies?"

"There were three of them. They were taken to Wright-Patterson Air Force Base near Dayton, Ohio. They're still there. Frozen solid all these years. The autopsy reports are fascinating. These creatures ... aliens ... have no visible internal organs. It was like cutting into a plant or a vegetable."

"But how are you involved in this? Roswell was long before your time or mine." *And how the hell did you know Roswell was one of the cases Morgen suggested I study? Is my apartment bugged? Have you been tapping my phone or reading my e-mail?*

"You are right. In fact, I only came into this game, as you call it, a little more than a decade ago when I left Brussels. And you've only been involved a matter of weeks. But what drew us both in started with the Roswell crash in 1947. Not the crash itself but the cover-up of the crash. It was handled so clumsily and the evidence of alien visitation at Roswell and in many later incidents was so obvious and ironclad that the top power structure, including Harry Truman, knew something had to be done. The concern was not that Roswell or UFO sightings should be kept secret. Truman and a handful of people around him knew that was impossible in a democracy with a free press.

"So, Truman appointed an ultra-top-secret panel of seven men to contain and control the growing UFO phenomenon.

Rather unimaginatively, they became known as The Seven to themselves and the people who work for them. Their dual agenda was to make UFOs, and the people who report them, objects of ridicule, and also to convince the public that the American government and other governments have way more knowledge of aliens and UFOs than they admit. They have even created widespread speculation, even belief among many, that the government is in league with the aliens, allowing them to abduct people and animals for experiments in exchange for alien technology. The Seven has worked very hard over the years to plant the notion in the public mind that the government knows what's going on and is in control."

Bill interrupted.

"I don't understand something. You speak of The Seven as though they are contemporary. But the ones Truman appointed must be dead by now. Earlier you said that most presidents don't know about this. Then who appoints new members to The Seven as they die or become too ill to serve?"

"Good question. The answer is that the group has the executive authority to select its own members independent of the White House or any other parts of the government. It also has virtually unlimited resources. Its budget is as black as black can get, hidden deep within other black budgets of the CIA and the NSA, as well as their counterparts in the other major industrialized nations. Only two presidents since Truman—Kennedy and Reagan—and a handful of foreign leaders have known of The Seven's existence.

"Reagan almost went off the rails in 1987, near the end of his second term. He was clearly suffering from the onset of Alzheimer's when he gave a speech at the United Nations in which he said differences among nations would vanish if we were facing an 'alien threat from outside this world.' Of course, because of the work of The Seven over the decades that comment was not taken seriously by anyone, especially the press. Rachel Maddow later dismissed it as one of the weirdest things he had ever said in public. We panicked a bit at first, but soon realized that his alien threat comment actually helped us. People either ridiculed it or saw it as further evidence of the government having secret knowledge of UFOs and aliens. Exactly what we wanted. But we took no chances. For the rest of Reagan's presidency his comments were closely controlled."

"Why does The Seven want to make people think the government knows more than it does, that it knows what's going on and is covering it up?"

"Ah, good reporter that you are, you've gone right to the heart of the matter. What the government wants to cover up is not what it knows, but what it doesn't know. It's the reverse of the X-Files."

"What do you mean?"

"Think back to Roswell. An alien spacecraft is flying around an area where the first atomic bomb was tested. It crashes within miles of a base that is housing nuclear facilities. It would be nice to know where it came from and what its occupants were up to. At first, some suspected it was some kind of secret Soviet operation. But Russians aren't four feet tall and hairless with big almond-shaped black eyes.

"What had to be kept secret then and what must be kept secret now, at all costs, is this: None of us—not the U.S. government, not the military, not any foreign governments nor their militaries—have a clue, not a clue, as to who these alien visitors are. Are you with me? There appear to be more than one species, and no one has any idea what they are up to. Let that sink in."

Colonel West's voice had grown weak. He pulled the paging device from his vest pocket and pressed the red button. Within seconds, the lock clicked and the door swung open. The same white-coated waiter who had served the food earlier walked into the room.

"Sir?"

"Could we get some coffee and some cookies or something sweet?"

"Right away, Sir."

As the waiter left the room, Colonel West looked at Bill.

The older man's flinty green eyes looked dull gray under the florescent lights. The skin under his eyes and on his cheeks had begun to sag a bit.

Bill broke eye contact and glanced around the room. *This is a sad, tortured man. No wonder. How many deaths has he been responsible for?*

Colonel West sighed and then started coughing.

"Excuse me," he said between coughs, "but I find that I tire easily these days. I'm just going to close my eyes and rest until the coffee arrives."

"No problem."

Colonel West cleared his throat and the coughing stopped; he lay back on the sofa, closed his eyes and appeared to go to sleep.

Bill tried to relax but couldn't. *Where the hell is Morgen? Is she in another room going through the same process with someone else? Who? What happened to Cindy's body? How do I know this guy is on the level? What happens when this is over? How can he prevent me from going public, especially with murders?*

In about ten minutes the waiter reappeared with a tray containing a silver pot of steaming coffee, two mugs, sugar, cream, and a bowl of sugar cookies. He sat the tray on the desk.

Colonel West opened his eyes and sat upright. He did not look rested.

"Will that be all, Sir? Shall I serve you?"

"No, thank you. That will be all for now."

The waiter nodded at Colonel West, turned, and left the room. The lock clicked as soon as he closed the door.

"Do you mind?" Colonel West asked, pointing toward the tray of coffee. "Black for me."

Bill poured two mugs of coffee, adding cream to his. He gave the mug of black coffee to Col. West. He sat the bowl of cookies on the small table between them.

"This sugar should give us some energy for a while, Bill. Are you ready to go on?"

"I guess."

*

"You're telling me that The Seven was created after Roswell to convince the public that the government secretly knows what's going on with UFO activity and may be in cahoots with aliens in exchange for advance technology?"

"Well, yes. But at the same time the government wanted to discredit, mainly through ridicule and disinformation, anyone who reported UFOs or took an interest in them. Those lights in the sky were planets, flares, or swamp gas. The witnesses were unreliable or were dreaming or hallucinating. So that people who go public with UFO sightings or abductions open themselves to ruinous ridicule. But in most cases, we leave just enough inconsistencies or 'evidence' that indicates the government knows more than it's telling. Slowly, over the years that has become the durable double narrative: ridicule on one level and the suspicion the government is hiding something on another. Which is what The Seven wants. Look at the polls. Millions claim to have witnessed UFOs. Most people think UFOs are real and their existence is part of a government cover-up. The former is true; the latter is pure fiction created by The Seven. Despite what the polls show, serious scientists want nothing publicly to do with UFOs. They know ridicule from the establishment could destroy their careers, not to mention their research grants. It's a delicate balancing act for The Seven. They want UFOs and aliens to be the objects of ridicule on one level to keep serious scientists away; they also want people to believe in a cover-up that indicates the government is in control and knows what's going on.

"The Majestic 12 document, which Morgen included in the cases she gave you to study, is a perfect example of The Seven at work. That document is a total fake created by The Seven in 1984 to make it appear that Truman formed a secret committee in 1947, code named Majestic 12, to oversee investigations and recovery of alien spacecraft. When the document was exposed as bogus, which The Seven orchestrated, the episode cast a negative light on the idea of such groups and gave The

Seven even deeper cover."

There he goes again, telling me something only Morgen and I know. He has to have bugged my apartment.

"Politicians also fear ridicule if they investigate UFOs or even take them seriously. Remember the flak Harry Reid took when it was disclosed that as Senate majority leader, he had convinced the Pentagon to spend twenty-two million dollars to investigate the UFO phenomena? Jimmy Carter became a laughingstock when he reported seeing a UFO. He went on to be elected president, mainly because of the public anger over Watergate and Gerald Ford's pardon of Nixon. The UFO story was almost as bad for Carter as his later claim that he was paddling a canoe when a big enraged rabbit attacked him. It's impossible to quantify, but a UFO and a rabbit had roles in making him a one-term president."

Carter and the UFO again. Were the trucks torched on the bridge to force me back to Jefferson or to keep me from reaching Walter Jansen in Atlanta? He saw the UFO with Carter. Warren Holden said Jansen was interested in UFOs, indicating that he might know something. Or have some secret files.

"I have a couple of questions. Did you stage the truck fires to scare me back to Jefferson or to keep me from reaching Atlanta and talking to Walter Jansen? Second, where is Cindy Watson's body? What in hell did she have to do with all this?"

"In the case of the bridge fires, a bit of both ... I guess. You have to realize that we were making this up as we went along, again thanks mainly to you, and I was faced with some out-of-control agents with too little oversight, too much money, and too many gadgets. As for the girl, her body was cremated at a military base in West Virginia. Her ashes were scattered in a nearby river. I'll tell you more about her as we move along."

"You don't seem very concerned about the death of a little girl. Or the murder of her father. Were you ever going to let Sharon Watson know her daughter was dead? Or just let her go to her grave tortured with doubt?"

"It would be too dangerous for us to contact her in any

way. The deaths of her daughter and husband, as well as that young reporter, are only three of many. As I said earlier, we all have to die."

What a cold fucker!

"Let me be sure I'm understanding you. The Seven manipulates public opinion to make UFOs and those who see them seem ridiculous, while at the same time creating a narrative that the government has some secret agreement with aliens and is somehow in control of what's going on?"

"That pretty much sums it up. All the government investigations of UFOs—Project Sign, Project Grudge, Project Blue Book, the Condon Report ... even that idiotic AATIP program that Harry Reid pushed for—were all generated and encouraged by The Seven as public relations ploys to cover up the truth. It's not hard to influence a U.S. senator. All it takes is money. You'd be surprised how little. Because of our success, journalistic accounts of UFOs and alien abductions are almost always mocking and superficial. You know what helped us the most? The success of the X-Files and Ancient Aliens on television. They really baked in the idea of a government conspiracy when the reality is just the opposite. And, hell, if supermarket tabloids didn't exist, we would've had to invent them.

"You may as well hear some more of the story, since you're not going to be repeating it to anyone. In addition to covering up our almost total lack of knowledge about the aliens, which we have done very successfully, The Seven is also trying to find out what they're up to. Our efforts at this have failed spectacularly.

"Not only have aliens been visiting the Earth for thousands of years, they've also established bases on the Moon and Mars. NASA, supposedly a civilian agency, became an arm of the military years ago and has since come under the control of The Seven. Why do you think we've never been back to the moon? NASA's main job right now is to cover up UFO bases and alien artifacts that have been photographed on the Moon and Mars by various space missions, some of them secret. Photographs of the so-called face on Mars were released in

1976 before The Seven controlled NASA. The 'face' was quickly labeled an optical illusion caused by shadows and light. The reported failure of the Mars Observer in 1993 was a lie. It functioned perfectly well for three years and sent back more photos that confirmed alien bases and craft on Mars."

"But what's all this got to do with a ten-year-old girl in Indiana?

"My main job for The Seven is to oversee the tracking of UFO sightings and adductions. As soon as the aliens release abductees we try to seize them and find out what was done to them. This is what happened to Cindy Watson after she was returned to her room from the UFO. We immobilized her parents with a short-acting sleeping gas; a locksmith's skills made it appear she ran away. But the shock of the original abduction, plus the powerful hypnotic drugs we gave her, proved too much for a ten-year-old. She died, as have some others in similar situations. As I said earlier, our agents killed Paul and the reporter. Lucky for you, I stepped in."

"But you people must have some suspicion or reason for what you're doing, some working hypothesis. What do you think you're looking for?"

"We suspect the aliens are abducting people in an effort to slowly alter the genetic makeup of the human race. Scientists working for The Seven speculate that the aliens may have interfered with human evolution in the far past. We know they have been visiting here for thousands, possibly hundreds of thousands, of years. Maybe they made some mistakes in the distant past that didn't become obvious until many thousands of years later. Maybe they are working to correct those errors. Perhaps humanity's tendency toward destructive aggression is the result of errors made in the genetic manipulation of primitive man. Or maybe they're extracting genetic material from humans for some use we have no clue about. We suspect they may have telepathic abilities.

"The bottom line is we don't know anything about UFOs or aliens for certain except that they exist. All we can do is speculate and try to find out. The Seven exists to hide our lack of knowledge and lack of control. No one knows who the aliens are, where they are from, or what they are doing. There seem to be several species of aliens, although the most common are the 'grays,' like the bodies we have from the Roswell crash: small, slender creatures with black, almond-shaped eyes. Others look pretty much like us only they are taller; a third group has reptilian features. Are they from other planets? From parallel universes? From the future? Are they competing or cooperating with each other? We don't know.

"All efforts to contact them have failed. Moves to interfere with them have proved disastrous and resulted in the destruction of aircraft, spacecraft, and crew. Unless provoked, they seem totally indifferent to human activity. Our last mission to the Moon was secret and the landing capsule was armed with laser weapons. It and its three-man crew were destroyed while in moon orbit preparing to land. In 1989, the aliens destroyed a Soviet spacecraft, Phobos 2, on a scientific mission to bombard the surface of Mars with laser beams in order to study the planet's topography. The aliens apparently viewed the craft as hostile. This led to the Mars Observer mission, which was carefully and very obviously designed as a photo reconnaissance craft; the aliens paid no attention to it."

Colonel West paused. He motioned for Bill to pour him another cup of coffee. He ate another cookie, chewing it slowly. He was clearly exhausted. His hand trembled as he took the cup of hot coffee from Bill.

Bill started to glance at his wristwatch but stopped himself when he again remembered Black Suit took it.

"What time is it?

Colonel West pulled his pocket watch from his vest.

"A little after three. Are you sleepy?"

"No."

"What do you think of my revelations so far?"

"My big question is why? Why not stop killing people and come clean. Add UFOs and the aliens to the long list of things we don't understand?"

"Think about it and consider the government's position.

Can you imagine what would happen if we were to confirm that UFO sightings and aliens are real? What if we said to the public: Yes, these craft and beings from we-don't-know-where routinely invade our air space, kidnap our citizens, mutilate our cattle, and we know nothing about the who or the why of any of this. We are powerless, absolutely powerless, to do anything. We don't know whether they are here for good for evil reasons. And, oh, by the way, we suspect they can read our minds and might be altering our genetic makeup. Can you imagine what would happen to the fabric of society? To religions? To government institutions? To government authority? To the stock market?

Bill took a sip of his coffee, which had grown lukewarm.

"I don't know. Why do you think the results of coming clean would be negative?"

"Because every study we have commissioned on the subject comes to that conclusion. NASA, Brookings, Rand ... they all have concluded that disclosing the reality of UFOs and aliens would disrupt the social order in ways from which we might never recover. And those conclusions were based on our solely revealing the reality of the aliens and do not take into account any disclosure of the fact that we don't know anything about them."

"Okay, I see your point of view. I don't agree with it, but I understand it. But why have you told me all this? And where is Morgen?"

"Morgen works for The Seven. I'm surprised you haven't figured that out by now."

Bill was stunned.

"I don't believe you."

"Believe me because it's true. Morgen's assignment was to make contact with you, introduce you a bit to the subject of extraterrestrials and then gently guide you here. All the while she made it seem like your idea. She's very good. She's also a bit of an adventure junkie, which you may have figured out by now. She also likes money, and we pay her well. She makes that story about living on a small inheritance with help from a roommate sound very convincing."

Bill's eyes began to burn as tears welled up in them. *This can't be true. This is not the Morgen I know and love.*

"But why me? Why didn't you just let your agents kill me?"

"Because I would like to recruit you. We could use someone with your skills and stature working behind the scenes for us. Like Morgen. With Morgen."

"Fuck you. No way. I want to talk to Morgen."

"Then you will never see or speak to Morgen again. She is presently on her way out of the country on one of our planes. You will not try to contact her. Ever."

"And who's going to stop me? Especially after I go public with the shit you're up to."

"Remember earlier that I told you that you would find it in your best interest to remain silent about what you have learned?"

Bill said nothing.

Colonel West stood up, leaning heavily on his cane. He walked around to the desk, took a key from a vest pocket, and opened the center drawer. From the drawer he pulled a manila file folder holding a thick stack of photocopies. He walked back to the sofa and eased himself onto the soft cushions.

He handed the file to Bill.

A few minutes later, after glancing at most of the copies in the folder, Bill knew that Colonel West was right. He would keep The Seven's secrets.

The file was full of documents that would prove to any reasonable person that Bill was an alcoholic and drug user who had been hospitalized several times over the past decade for treatment of paranoid schizophrenia and delusions. Included were statements and diagnoses from psychiatrists, along with hospital bills and canceled checks showing payments by Bill's insurance company. Although total fiction, release of this file could ruin him. There would be no defense; any attempt to refute it would only make it seen truer.

Bill wiped his eyes and sighed.

Colonel West leaned forward.

"You, better than anyone, know what the press would do with this. We're covered if reporters try to check out the accuracy of much of this stuff. But you know as well as I that most won't check. They'll accept the documents as solid evidence. Those few who might check will stop once one document is confirmed as true. Remember what you'll be trying to prove. You'll go down the UFO black hole like so many others. Just bringing up the subject will open you to ridicule and damage your reputation; these documents will destroy it."

"So, what now?"

"You can reconsider our offer to work for us. If you still refuse, we'll take you home and you can resume your life. The choice is yours."

"There's no way I would work for you."

Colonel West stood up and walked to the door, limping heavily.

He turned to Bill.

"In a few minutes, someone will bring your belongings and the black hood, which you must wear until you are delivered to your apartment building.

Colonel West unlocked the door.

"Goodbye, Mr. Sanders."

CHAPTER 30

"Bill, you seem distracted. Is something wrong?"

Gerald, their usual waiter, was struggling to lower a venetian blind to block the late October sun flooding their table at Dave's.

"No. I'm just worn out from all those radio and TV interviews. Plus, my hand is sore from all those book signings."

Nancy Luke smiled.

"Well, think of the money. You'll feel better."

Bill and Nancy were having their regular lunch a month after the publication of *Look Down*. It got rave reviews, as Nancy had predicted, and immediately soared to the top of The New York Times bestseller list. As Nancy also had predicted, the Hollywood producer doubled his offer to a million dollars for the film rights to *Look Down*.

Yeah, the money's nice. But it won't bring back Jane or let me forget Morgen. I guess I should hate her for betraying me, but I can't.

"What are you going to do next, when all the publicity around *Look Down* eases off?"

"I think I'll start work on the Middle East book I've been talking about. Maybe head there in the spring and see what happens."

"I think that's a good book idea, and I think you'll have another winner on your hands like *Points South*. But you'll be gone a long time, and I'll miss our lunches."

"I'll be gone for several months, at least. But I'll make a couple of trips back during that time. I'll have to spend some time in D.C., too."

Gerald brought their soup and refilled their wine glasses.

"So, did things get resolved from your trip to Indiana? You said you would explain it to me at some point."

"Yes and no. They never did find any trace of Paul's daughter, Cindy. Sharon, that's Paul's wife, moved to Indianapolis this summer to be near her parents. She kept the house in Jefferson. I'm not sure why. Our last phone conversation did not go well. She somehow blames me for Paul's death. I can't explain it."

"How can she blame you? You went there to help."

"I don't know. She wasn't being rational. But I can understand. She lost her husband and daughter. Maybe I'll try to get in touch with her at Christmas."

Or maybe not. I don't really want to get involved again, especially since I know what happened to Cindy. And Paul.

By the time the main course arrived, Nancy was discussing details of the movie deal.

After lunch, Bill took a taxi back to his apartment.

He sat at his desk, sorting through a stack of mail. Most of it he threw away. The rest he put into a wicker basket.

He went to the kitchen to get a drink of water.

Back at his desk, he opened the center drawer and removed a manila envelope containing three items: Paul's cabin key, which he had forgotten to return to Sharon; a short newspaper clipping from the Times; and a creamy white envelope with his name handwritten on the front.

The clipping was the obituary of Colonel Richard West that ran in August. It mentioned his work at NATO in Brussels where he was a communications specialist and listed his hometown as Chicago. No current address. No survivors. No services. Cause of death was pancreatic cancer. He died at a hospital in Maryland. He was seventy-two years old.

An unidentified person had left the white envelope on George's desk in the lobby two days after Bill, hooded, was driven back to his apartment following his meeting with

Colonel West. Inside was a matching piece of paper containing two handwritten words: "I'm sorry." It was signed "M."

Bill pressed the note to his face. On the paper were dried drops of Morgen's musky perfume.

— The End —

THE TRILOGY

Book 2

SHADOWS

coming Fall 2020

Bill Sanders reluctantly returns to his hometown of Jefferson, Indiana, where he makes an astonishing discovery about his and Paul's Watson's pasts. This, along with a letter from a dead man that discloses shocking information about his wife's death, sets him on a collision course with The Seven.

Book 3

SECRETS

coming Spring 2021

Bill Sanders and Morgen Remley are reunited and join forces in an effort to stop The Seven that takes them all the way to the Oval Office.

About the Author

Fred Ellis Brock is the author of the best-selling *Retire on Less Than You Think: The New York Times Guide to Planning Your Financial Future* (2nd Edition – Times Books/Henry Holt, 2008); *Health Care on Less Than You Think: The New York Times Guide to Getting Affordable Coverage* (Times Book/Henry Holt, 2006); and *Live Well on Less Than You Think: The New York Times Guide to Achieving Your Financial Freedom* (Times Books/Henry Holt, 2005). For more than a decade he was a business editor and columnist at The New York Times. For six years he wrote that paper's "Seniority" column and was the author of the "Off the Rack" media column prior to that. He has also worked as an editor and reporter for The Wall Street Journal, The Houston Chronicle and The Louisville Courier-Journal. He holds an M.Ed. from Temple University and a B.A. in English literature from Hanover College. He has taught undergraduate and graduate reporting and editing at New York University and Kansas State University, where he held the R.M. Seaton Professional Journalism Chair. He was a fellow at the Washington Journalism Center, with a concentration in public affairs reporting. He lives in Arizona, where he teaches at the University of Arizona and is a contributor to The New York Times and a featured speaker for the Times Journeys travel program. He is represented by the David Black Literary Agency and AEI Speakers Bureau.

Brock, while pursuing conventional journalism and teaching careers, has been interested in UFO sightings and science fiction since he was in high school. He is a member of the Mutual UFO Network (MUFON) and has witnessed unexplained sightings in the U.S. and Europe. He has interviewed scores of witnesses to UFO sightings for both articles and personal research; he has read widely on the subject. This is reflected in the authenticity of *The Seven*.

CPSIA information can be obtained
at www.ICGtesting.com
Printed in the USA
JSHW010722220120
3684JS00001B/1

9 781948 018777